Necron: Beyond Einstein's Barrier

By Oliver Strong

Smashwords Edition

ISBN: 978-0-9575457-4-8

Word Count: 28,148

Contents

Chapter One

Victor gazed into the void ... there it was again, a point of light arched, a bow string drawn taught on its missile ... then it vanished. Travelling to meet gruesome fate beyond the speed of light, Einstein's rules of time dilation shattered. Rather than five years at near light speed then decelerating to find thirty had passed on Earth, they travelled beyond a barrier considered unbreakable in the 20th century, proven otherwise by the 27th century. Super computers micro-managed laws of physics, five years passed as five minutes at the rendezvous.

Victor whiled away personal time seizing brief glimpses of starlight, universal gatekeepers exposed their divine frame just for him as the S.S. Charon defied atomic age physics.

A young lady stood on her toes observing ancient light trapped between Einstein and Necron Industries training vessel, 'Read your file?'

Victor didn't turn away, 'I did.'

'Notice anyone?'

'I shouldn't have looked.'

Diana, a bright young girl of twenty eight years on death, defied old world science along with thousands more hurtling on the razor edge of time, 'Come on, we're drinking before basic training starts.'

'I think I'll pass.'

'Come on Vic.'

He focused on flashing bows of light, bright bridges spanning the distance between him and normal time. Victor need only travel its luminous crescent to return to his previous life, the stars both beckoned and taunted in equal measure.

'I guess you'll be dwelling in self-pity. If you change your mind I'm getting drunk in the Mess until downtime.'

Victor grabbed her cold necrotic hand, Diana Zeng had been a good friend ever since this journey beyond death began, 'Forgive me, it's hit me hard.'

'It hit us all hard, but try to enjoy the here and now,' she pulled his attention from the porthole and into the Mess.

My woes began more than five years ago, I lived in New York, I had a family, a wife and two kids along with some crushing tax bills, in about a month we'd be destitute. One night I went over the galactic net and through a bottle of vodka looking for anything I might grasp onto. Scams and schemes were ten to the penny, you know, crap about winning the Epsilon A lottery, just forward ten thousand in fees and we'll send you your cheque for five million Epsilon Tax Rights, rich relatives etcetera, I was dumb but not that dumb. My wife didn't know about my … our troubles, I'd spent my, our tax rights on gifts for her and good times for me instead of paying local government its extortion fee.

'Why don't you come to bed honey?'

'Just a few minutes … say have you ever heard of Necron Industries?'

My wife leapt out of bed like there was a fire under it, 'Turn it off Victor, you don't wanna go anywhere near those brain butchers!'

'It seems pretty equitable. They pay any outstanding debts and look after your family once you've died.'

'In exchange for your body!'

Victor turned to face his wife, 'But I'd be dead, it's not like I'd care.'

'What about your family, burying an empty coffin while they butcher you on a slab, I couldn't bare it.'

'Don't worry it was just a thought.'

'Are you coming to bed now?'

'Sure,' he hit the send button delivering a request to Necron Industries.

The next morning Victor arose before his wife, a hologramatic monitor silently flashed. He tapped the soft rubber keyboard opening a message board. A beautiful smiling lady greeted Victor, 'Good morning, your application has been accepted. Necron Industries would appreciate a face to face meeting with one of our representatives.'

A list of interview slots popped up for the rest of the week, 'Please select a convenient time slot.'

Victor selected a slot during his lunch break, 'Thank you, you now have an interview with Necron Industries at one thirty this afternoon at our nearest office in Central Park, please be punctual,' her image disappeared. His wife groaned searching for the cold part of the pillow. Victor wiped sweat from his brow … little did he know this heart rendering moment would not be the last.

That afternoon Victor entered an atmosphere breaking tower that was the Trump Sky Lift, an orbital elevator exclusive to high profile occupants prepared to pay grotesque rental fees. The year was 2682, humanity populated several close by star systems in its first attempt to make a mark on the galaxy. Yet like all well planned and carefully co-ordinated government endeavours … it had gone tits up.

Victor checked in at reception, his work buddies warned against Necron, told him he'd have to be crazy to sign up, yet they didn't have the government mafia poised to take his apartment, throw him in prison and leave his wife and kids on the streets.

'Mr Zellmann?' said an attractive receptionist.

'Yes,' replied Victor rising from a comfortable seat.

'Doctor Kaufman is ready to see you now,' she gestured toward her left, 'third room to your right.'

As Victor walked past her desk she smiled, 'I hope you'll be staying with us Mr Zellmann.'

He nodded his head and continued until reaching a placard stating the Doctor's name, before he might press the bell a German accent emanated from within, 'You may enter Mr Zellmann.'

Inside Victor was greeted by a spic and span surgery room, a short man with a bald streak and glasses stood hand extended.

They shook hands, 'Please sit Mr Zellmann.'

The Doctor pulled files from his memory banks, examining Victor's medical records via hologram. Victor wondered how they obtained his medical information since not even corporations were authorised access.

'Yes, yes, very good Mr Zellmann, have you abused your body in any way since your previous medical?'

Victor felt a little violated, 'Certainly not!'

Kaufman peered over his glasses, 'Then you won't protest if I certify your honesty?'

'Well that's hardly a way to treat someone …'

'Mr Zellmann, no offence is intended, please understand this is a treacherous business, we must balance risk against reward and Necron Industries is taking all the risk. Besides that I have every bum, heroin fiend and solvent abuser in New York City lining up to strike a deal. Not to be terribly blunt they aren't our ideal clientele.'

The atmosphere of Kaufman's surgery began to stifle, 'I'm sorry I was just shocked to see you possess my medical records.'

Kaufman smiled, 'A little grease on the wheels of bureaucracy gets the machine moving along its correct path.'

'So can you help me?'

'First I want you to understand exactly what we do here; we are the largest cryogenics company in the galaxy today. We freeze your body, harvest its organs, tissue, nerves, hair follicles … anything salvageable then auction it on … usually after you're dead,' Victor's eyes widened, 'ONLY JOKING!' Kaufman laughed yet Victor's breathing tightened.

'I understand that but what about my tax bill?'

Kaufman made a grim expression, upset that his moment of comedy was brought to an abrupt end, 'Yes well, once we confirm you're not a fiend our computers will assess the net worth of your corpse on today's market. Afterwards we will make an offer, you may accept or refuse, if you accept RFID nanites shall be injected into your bloodstream so if you require an ambulance you'll be sent to the nearest hospital with a Necron Industries cryogenics facility.'

'You mean if I'm already dead.'

Kaufman locked eyes, 'We need to freeze you ASAP Mr Zellmann but have my assurance you will not be frozen until pronounced dead by a physician.'

'Provided it's not a Necron physician!'

Kaufman gave a big belly laugh, 'Very good Mr Zellmann but I'm afraid not, if we had to factor in legal costs such as law suits we might as well sign up bums. No, we need healthy compliant corpses Mr Zellmann, why I myself have a plan with Necron Industries.'

'So that's it I sign my corpse over to you and you pay my tax bill?'

'If everything goes as it should, yes,' Kaufman paused, the room was quiet for a few seconds, 'Perhaps there is something else I might interest you in?'

'You do tea and biscuits?'

'Please bear with me a moment, Necron Industries has a new project to be launched next year. If your corpse qualifies for the plan you'll get extended benefits.'

'I'll be dead, how would I get extended benefits?'

'Your surviving family, wife and direct blood children would receive a cheque from Necron Industries each month.'

'If my corpse qualifies?'

'And that assessment can only be made on death.'

'Are you signed up for it?'

'In fact I am although I may not qualify anymore.'

'Why?'

'Hmm, it's complicated but a young man below the age of thirty will certainly qualify, provided his corpse has only minimal damage.'

'Okay hit me with it Doc.'

A hologram jumped out from the desk, a beautiful young lady dressed in military hot pants, perfect make up, red lips, long blonde hair displayed an attractive smirk, 'Have you ever desired to journey the stars? Discover new species? Engage in alien cultures beyond your wildest imagination?' she pulled a large assault rifle from out of shot, 'Then blow the motherfuckers back to the shithole they came from?' she fired her weapon to the sound of alien screams, foreign howls hit a crescendo before dying down. She rested the smoking weapon on her hip, tossed a perfectly sculpted hairdo back in place then continued, 'And all the time keep those you love financially solvent? Then Project Necron has a place for you,' the picture faded to a large space cruiser perhaps a battleship, Victor couldn't tell without another object to provide scale, its engines lit up behind. The vessel was different from the standard sleek military cruisers and battleships in news releases, this was a block with smaller blocks attached to it, the only thing discerning its fore and aft were massive engines at one end and a group of long thin constructions protruding out the fore end. As the camera swung around the vessel's insignia appeared, rather unusual since all military vessels were entirely black for obvious reasons. This ship had painted in large white letters "S.S. NECRON".

Victor was confused, 'What on Earth was that about?'

'I'm sure you're aware of the war in the colonies, yes?'

'And?'

'Well at Necron Industries we believe there is profit in conflict.'

'How's that?'

'Oh there are many engagements resulting in derelict space ships on both sides. Colonies pay very well for assistance when their government is unable to offer tax funded protection,' he laughed.

'I heard all nations agreed to rule ... forty something, it was announced by the President, right?'

Kaufman nodded, 'Rule forty eight Mr Zellmann but when a legion of seven foot psychopaths are closing in to murder your children, the President's words are worth very little insurance ... not that they're worth anything on Earth.'

'So what's this got to do with me, I mean I'll be dead right?'

The Doctor placed a legal document on the desk, 'This is totally optional, the space cruiser you witnessed is Project Necron, we intended to man it and profiteer, for want of a better word.'

'And some bimbo with a gun is supposed to convince me, come on I'm not that dumb, I've heard about what goes on out there, besides the journey to the nearest colony is like ten years at near light speed, my family would be thirty years old before I even got there!'

'First of all if you're dead it wouldn't matter, second we intend to get around time dilation by travelling beyond light speed.'

'That's not possible!'

'We did it six months ago Mr Zellmann. Necron mastered faster than light travel, we are already licensing it to others, civilian pigeon carriers are being upgraded with FTL as we speak. Necron Industries possess the only military vessel able to travel beyond Einstein's barrier!'

'So what does this have to do with me and making extra money for my family?'

'Necron intends to widen profit margins, if a colony is in trouble the colonists will send an FTL carrier pigeon delivering a distress message. The S.S. Necron will respond within minutes, repel the enemy and claim any salvage. The only snag being that time dilation at faster than light is the inverse of near light speed.'

'You mean time travels slower for the crew rather than everyone else?'

'That is why we intend to crew the Necron with the deceased. They may spend years training for a single engagement to arrive a minute after the carrier pigeon departed and strike the enemy, without aging a day.'

'But I'm not dead.'

'You will be, we all will be, and if your corpse fits parameters you will be revived and take your place on the Necron.'

'I didn't know they could revive people after death.'

'Not entirely, we're still working on it Mr Zellmann, in fact it may never happen.'

'What do you mean?'

'Many have no memory of their past, training them for even the simplest duty is a great task, post reanimation.'

A nurse entered the room, 'Mr Zellmann has passed toxicology.'

'Thank you,' he pushed two documents forward.

Victor examined the documents, signed the first by placing his palm upon the tablet. It scanned his prints, blood vessels and DNA. Victor hesitated over the Project Necron tablet while a nurse injected RFID nanites into his blood stream.

'What the hell,' Victor signed it, 'I'm twenty two, married with two kids, I wake up most mornings feeling like a zombie as it is!'

Kaufman laughed, 'That's the spirit young man!' he tapped his desk, 'There you go your tax arrears are no longer a problem Mr Zellmann.'

Victor let out a sigh of relief, he was keeping his home, his wife would only discover the truth after he'd croaked, heh, she'd have to bitch at someone else this time, besides Victor wasn't planning on kicking the bucket before forty years of age so from his perspective it was win, win.

That was eight years before I was hit by a car and knocked into a coma. Necron improved its technology and I'm making the journey to Tau Ceti. Boot camp is five years. I'll arrive five minutes after I left from the galaxy's point of view. It'll be five years on this ship but since I'm already dead I guess I don't have to worry about losing my youthful looks. We regenerate in what look like traditional sleeper booths used for suspended animation during the long haul to the colonies.

Everyone is scrambling to achieve faster than light however we're the only people with a crew and vessels fully fitted for it.

A bell went off, lights changed colour, 'Boot camp starts today!' said Diana in an excited tone.

Victor followed her into an office where queues of men and women were sorted. Improved revival technology meant recruits retained much of their past skills, ex-pilots, medics, engineers and technicians filled the room. Victor was an architect in his former life, not much use aboard a military vessel. He and Diana were directed down a corridor with Marines written above its doorway. She smiled at him happy to see the first face to greet her after death.

Dressed in matching grey jump suits dazed recruits filed into a purpose built gymnasium, more than two thousand men and women resurrected from hibernation awaited fate.

A detachment of men clad in dark combat armour held assault rifles, berets on heads. A Drill Sergeant crossed his arms. A senior officer observed their uncoordinated shuffle into the centre from a raised gantry.

Victor recognised a white symbol plastered on the left breast of each Marine's armour, crossed assault rifles below a skull wearing a beret. The woman in Kaufman's office, on the recruiting video, wore the exact emblem.

'ATTENTION! OFFICER ON THE DECK!' screamed the Drill Sergeant.

Men and women in plain grey trousers and shirts looked gormlessly at one another some shrugging shoulders in an undefined stupor, awaiting a judge to appear and pronounce sentence for the crime of death.

Marines dressed in black combat armour stamped the floor in concert, rifles held across chests and eyes forward.

'I SAID ATTENTION, THAT MEANS YOU ASSHOLES TOO!' bellowed the Sergeant.

The group of two thousand or so made a motley sight attempting to follow directions while lamenting their situation.

Sergeant Murray moved closer, he halted when the officer above spoke, 'Welcome to Project Necron, I'm sure you all have plenty of questions so I'll make it easy and put the majority to rest now,' the man spoke in an American accent that somehow matched his miserable demeanour. His eye fawned upon recruits, a man made by the U.S. Marine Corps, reincarnated by science, he was the embodiment of the Necron Marine, 'Yes you are dead, yes you are now property of Necron Industries. The only way to quit is via harvesting, where upon your corpse will be dissected for the use of those in active service.

If there are any further questions each one of you will be furnished with a copy of the contract he or she signed.

That ladies and gentlemen is the long story, the short story is that I own you and from now on I will not tolerate any bullshit is that understood?'

A young man broke out in uncontrollable laughter he could have been no more than twenty years of age, the poor guy, dead at twenty and revived to suffer an eternal hell in space.

The officer nodded, Drill Sergeant Murray strode up to the young man and snapped his neck.

'He will be harvested, his family will no longer receive any benefits from Necron Industries as per our contract,' stated the officer, 'does anyone else find their situation humorous?'

The entire hall fell silent as a graveyard.

'Excellent, my name is Major Flatley, you may refer to me as Major or sir, understood?'

'YES SIR!' replied the new recruits.

Major Flatley grinned, 'Excellent, you will be spending the next five years travelling beyond Einstein's barrier. During this period you shall be trained to fight your enemy. You will receive instruction twenty hours per standard Earth day, four hours you may recreate. The following twenty four hours will be spent at rest in regeneration capsules. You must regenerate your necrotic cells every twenty four hours, otherwise decay will set in and if allowed to continue past seventy two hours re-animation may no longer be an option. If this occurs in the line of duty your family will continue to receive benefits from Necron Industries, and yes you can die a second time,' Major Flatley walked out the area.

Chapter Two

Clad in grey uniforms reminiscent of a communist prison camp, Victor and Diana drank together in the Mess.

The gravity of their situation sunk in as vodka slowly slipping down a cold glass. Cursed to serve an army of dead, no-one expected or wished to be here, it was too much to absorb in a single day.

Victor had been furnished with his file upon resurrection, faces he saw during regeneration, occupying the swirling mist of death, began to make sense. Only on reading did it become clear that never again would Victor see his children. His wife buried a coffin decorated with his name six feet beneath the earth.

His career was flourishing alongside a loving family until at the age of thirty Victor was hit by a vehicle after its AI lost control. Three weeks in a coma and he was pronounced deceased. Despite her best attempts to prevent it Necron Industries claimed her husband's corpse, he was plunged into a vat of liquid helium and transported to the nearest facility for assessment.

On discovering a contract with Project Necron staff thoroughly examined the remains. Victor's blood drained in exchange for a nanite solution, quadrillions of microscopic machines replaced blood cells, organs certified and fortified. Slowly the subject thawed, chemical computers observing each minute nuance his corpse produced.

Upon reaching -100 °C Victor was transferred inside a regeneration chamber to revitalise necrotic tissue. Brain functions read positive, heart, lungs and everything else normalised. Next he was shipped aboard S.S. Charon, the boatman who in mythology carried dead from the banks of the Styx into Hades domain.

When required she hauled anchor to rendezvous with S.S. Necron delivering reinforcements to the front lines on the edge of settled space. Not every man and woman dreaming in their regeneration booth was successfully revived, it was hit and miss.

Though the majority were reanimated perhaps only 10% made their destination end. The greatest casualties amongst Marines whereas Technical staff fared best, they possessed skills before death, it's easier to train a dead man in something he did as a career in life. Yet moulding raw recruits without military experience into the galaxies most diligent killers was no simple task. If 10% of recruits had not been harvested by the time they reached S.S. Necron, Flatley considered it a success.

'So Vic ... you smiled when you were alive?' asked Diana in a sardonic tone.

'Yeh, I did.'

'What made you smile?'

'Stuff.'

'What stuff?'

'I don't know, stuff.'

Diana plonked her drink on the table, 'I guess Sartre was right.'

Victor pulled back from a town called misery, 'Sorry, who?'

'Sartre.'

'Who's he?'

'A French philosopher.'

'So what's he right about?'

'Hell is other people.'

'I guess if all my friends were French I'd agree.'

Diana smiled, 'Now that's funny.'

'I was being serious.'

'Jesus Christ you can be depressing!'

'You mean there's something else to be depressed about other than the fact we're dead and signed up to camp Nazi?'

'I used to go to bars and guys would hit on me, it felt good to be a piece of meat every now and again. Sitting with you is like trying to get fucked by a castrated lettuce.'

'Sorry.'

'Stop apologising it's getting annoying.'

'Sorry.'

She knocked back her drink in frustration, 'Want another?'

'No, I'm good thanks,' he fell back into a trance, staring into approaching oblivion, his future fixed, death encompassed on every side. Victor saw loneliness and misery gathering pace as space ship Charon hurtled toward the abyss.

'Hey Vic, you okay?'

Victor snapped out unaware how long he'd gazed at nothing, 'Sure.'

'What you thinking about?'

'Nothing.'

'Every time I look you're staring at the wall.'

'I think about my family, what happens to them and then I think about myself and what'll become of me.'

'Urrhhhh,' grunted Diana in a disparaging tone.

'Something wrong?'

'Always thinking about yourself.'

He shrugged, 'What else is there?'

'What about thinking of me?'

'I don't understand.'

'Don't you think I'm pretty?'

'Sure I do.'

'So?'

'So?'

'Jesus, do I have to spell it out?'

'Maybe he could whisper it in my ear.'

'I would very much appreciate it if you drink up and screw my brains out until we have to regenerate, understand?'

A man aged about twenty swaggered up to their table, 'Hey there babe, if he ain't man enough why don't you let me show you a good time?'

Diana peered at the cocky fellow, his juvenile buddies egging him on, 'Go fuck yourself loser.'

His friends laughed yet he persisted, 'You know why they call me coffee?'

Diana replied with sarcasm in her delicate voice, 'Please tell me before I explode in anticipation.'

The fellow moved his hips to his buddies approval, 'Because only I've got that long slow grind baby.'

Without another word she grabbed his nuts and squeezed hard, he dropped his drink scrambling to remove her iron grip yet the more he struggled the tighter she squeezed.

Diana smirked, 'You want to find out why they call me nutcracker … I'll give you a clue, it has nothing to do with Tchaikovsky.'

'Okay lady,' rasped a young Don Juan, 'I get it.'

Diana released his testicles, 'Maybe they should call you decaf from now on?' he staggered into to his howling friends. Victor displayed a confused expression asking why she'd done such a thing.

'Dying did not remove my standards. So what about my offer?'

'I'm flattered, really.'

'But?'

'Would you walk with me?'

'Fine,' she knocked her vodka down, 'let me wash my hands first.'

They strolled down one of many armour plated corridors lining Charon's outer hull, the only area he could find a window on the ship. Stopping at a small porthole Victor watched for light, sure enough a star exploded into a curve then disappeared, 'Did you see that?'

'Yeh,' replied an unimpressed Diana.

'Souls of the dead crying out across the void, our souls Diana.'

'Who told you that load of shit?'

'I don't know, a face in my dreams, I've never seen her before, maybe I'll recall who she is later.'

'Well this is charming,' she turned her palm to the ceiling viewing a multipurpose device attached to her wrist, it scanned her body, gave relative time, schedule alerts and right now it told her regeneration was required in fifty two minutes, 'How about fucking my brains out first then watching the stars?'

Victor turned and embraced Diana, she thought this was it, but he began to weep clutching tighter and tighter.

'What's wrong Vic?'

'I'm empty.'

'You need another drink?'

'Inside Diana, my soul is dead.'

'Newsflash Vic, we're all dead.'

'I've lost my past, in exchange for a barren future, don't you feel the same?' She locked eyes in a steeled gaze powerful enough to crush an automobile, 'My family was poor, we lived in Hong Kong. Everyone clamoured to sign up with Necron, radiation caused birth defects and cell decay others were heroin fiends. Most of my family died in that cursed city.'

'So how did you die?'

Diana lowered her collar to reveal a horrific scar spanning her dainty neck, 'Triads.'

'I'm sorry.'

'Will you stop telling me you're sorry! My shitty life wasn't your fault, it wasn't my fault,' her voice became soft, 'I want to make the most of my death, if that makes any sense?'

He nodded his head, 'As crazy as that sounds it does, and I do find you attractive in fact you're the only person I really want to be with on this ship.'

She stood on tip toes kissing his lips, her cold necrotic flesh touched his and in that zero sum equation somewhere, somehow a spark of life ignited between them. Her brown opal eyes met the green of his, colours passing through a solemn sheen of death as sunlight through grey clouds on a winter day.

Victor felt it within, something he'd only experienced as a living person, when looking into Diana's bleared eyes passion warmed his heart, 'Thank you.'

'We haven't fucked yet.'

'You've done more than that; I can feel something deep inside, something I haven't felt for a long time.'

She folded her arms and lamented, 'That's what I was hoping for.'

Victor embraced her … they kissed again but with greater intensity, two soulless corpses cursed to a future of eternal hell, created passion aboard a ship of the dead sailing beyond Einstein's barrier to meet terrible fate.

Twenty four hours later a deck of regeneration units opened in concert, a thick mist spilled out before occupants rose, Diana gave Victor a little wave.

He smiled back considering that if she weren't dead Diana would be glowing like the morning sun right now.

 Whilst regenerating Victor witnessed haunting faces, Diana's recollection was far clearer, probably because he'd suffered a head wound before death. Victor wondered that if he possessed her recollection would those faces be nightmares or warm memories to reminisce over.

 Victor rose from his regeneration unit feeling rather stiff. Diana walked straight over to him and held his hand, 'Last night was great.'

 The pair kissed as others rolled out booths. The Drill Sergeant, another Necron made man, approached as they rubbed noses, 'Well, well, well,' he removed a cheap cigar from his mouth, 'looks like we got a pair of lovebirds.'

 'Are there rules against kissing?' inquired Victor.

 'Only if you kiss me son,' cackled Sergeant Murray, 'On the deck in twenty minutes, last man to report in gets latrine duty!'

 'Yes sir,' Diana held Victor's yanking him on deck.

 Standing to attention the last man made it in, 'RECRUIT WHAT'S YOUR NAME!' screamed Murray.

 He looked around then back at the Sergeant, 'Me?'

 'THAT'S "ME, SIR" YOU USELESS HUNK OF SHIT!'

 'Errm, me sir?'

 A ripple of laughter fell over the deck, 'SHUT UP! YOU WILL SPEAK WHEN SPOKEN TO, UNDERSTOOD?'

 'Yes sir,' replied his motley recruits.

 'WHAT WAS THAT?'

 'Yes sir.'

 'MY GRANDMA MAKES MORE NOISE ON THE SHITTER THAN ALL OF YOU LOSERS PUT TOGETHER!'

 'YES SIR!'

 'That's better, now you what's your name?'

 'Bonaparte, sir,' he replied in a French accent.

 'Come here!'

 The young man who could be no more than twenty one walked up to the Drill Sergeant in a slouch.

 'ATTENTION BONAPARTE.'

The young lad stood up straight.

'You French son?'

'Yes sir.'

'Like Napoleon.'

The young man furrowed his brow.

'Napoleon Bonaparte.'

'I'm sorry I do not know this person, sir.'

Recruits sniggered amongst themselves, 'SHUT UP!'

Chuckles died off as quickly as they began, 'So you're ignorant AND lazy!'

Bonaparte shrugged his shoulders.

Sergeant Murray spoke to one of the armed soldiers in jet black combat gear, 'PRIVATE MORLEY, WHAT IS THE PROPER RESPONSE TO MY STATEMENT?'

'YES SIR, SIR.'

Bonaparte smirked, 'Yes sir, sir.'

Before the deck might respond to Bonaparte's humorous reply Sergeant Murray placed an arm around Bonaparte's head, resting a palm on his forehead, the other hand firmly clasped the lad's shoulder and in a single move his spinal cord was broken, cutting bodily communication with the brain. Bonaparte collapsed to the deck, involuntary twitches contorted his expression between sinister laughter and a painful grimace.

'PRIVATE MORLEY!'

'YES SIR!'

'Take this corpse to harvesting his contract with Project Necron is now terminated.'

'Understood sir.'

Two men in combat gear secured weapons and dragged the lad away much to Victor's shock.

Murray took a drag on his cigar, blowing out smoke he sneered, 'DOES ANYONE ELSE WISH TO JOIN BONAPARTE?'

Silence filled the deck.

'IN THAT CASE YOU ARE THE PROPERTY OF PROJECT NECRON, YOU WILL DO WHAT I SAY, WHEN I SAY AND YOU WILL BE PUNCTUAL, LACK OF PUNCTUALITY IS NOT TOLERATED ON THIS SHIP, UNDERSTOOD?'

'YES SIR!' the deck began to shape up, slouchers coming to attention, recruits moving into ordered rows.

'Now that we understand each other it's time for basic training, today you'll take a series of basic fitness tests, the corporation has to assess viability of your body in combat. Any dropouts will be harvested, so get your heart pumping or it'll be given to someone that can, understood?'

'YES SIR!'

Twenty hours later Diana and Victor met in the Mess, many men and women arrived in harvesting that day. Victor hadn't run since school and he'd certainly not run a marathon before, but the crunch of necks provided adequate motivation to push the limits, he came in among the top 10% along with Diana.

One oddity was the fact he didn't feel hot or sweat, nanites in his body managed temperature, holding heat within until it was time to urinate. Once Victor did urinate his penis burnt as hot urine steamed out in one go, a whole marathon's worth.

Diana brought over two vodkas, holding her glass up she waited for Victor to do likewise, 'A toast.'

'To what?'

'To surviving basic fitness.'

'I'll drink to that,' they toasted before downing the liquor.

Diana had managed to acquire a small quarter bottle of vodka from the bar, she poured a second round and let out a sigh before slouching into her chair, 'I'm dead tired.'

Victor chuckled, 'Now that's funny.'

She closed her eyes as the irony dawned, 'Yeh, I guess I could do stand up or something.'

'Too tired for another midnight stroll on the outer decks?'

'I cannot fuck.'

'Basic fitness took it out of you?' Victor displayed a cheeky smile.

'I was fine until I pissed ... think about it Einstein.'

Victor thought on the workings of the female body for a moment, it didn't take a brain surgeon to understand Diana's loss of libido, 'I've got it, sorry.'

'What about you?'

'To be honest it's throbbing like my Grandpa's ass after he had major piles surgery, I never want to take a piss again.'

Diana had an adorable smile, despite gaunt grey death she lightened up his life. She raised her glass again, 'To your Grandpa's ass and the memories we retain.'

Victor tapped glasses then stopped; he'd remembered his Grandpa's operation from when he was a small boy. He recalled nothing of that old man until now, a distant face in the dense mist of his past had become more defined; regeneration was a little less frightening and all thanks to Diana.

'What's wrong?'

'Oh nothing, I just remembered by Grandfather.'

'Really?'

Other men and women in the Mess looked over at Victor, mumbling under their breath.

'Yeh, I saw his face in my dreams, until now I had no idea he was my Grandfather.'

'To new memories!' Diana took another drink.

Members of the Mess patted him on the back, congratulating Victor on recovering a piece of his history.

Chapter Three

A metal sheet exposed the interior of his regeneration unit to the ceiling's white glare. Twenty four hours of regeneration prevented the inevitable aches and pains expected in life. His legs swung over the side to touch a cold metal floor, cold to a living organism, body temperature to him.

Over the past two days a small amount of recruits were harvested, literally ten or twenty due to biological problems missed by doctors on Earth, perhaps this wasn't going to be as tough as he thought?

Diana arose, her glowing complexion lessened Victor's anxiety, warming his ice cold heart.

'Have fun with your girlfriend last night,' cackled Sergeant Murray over a cheap cigar.

Victor narrowed his eyes, 'She was very pleasant company, thank you Sergeant.'

'Then you better hope she makes it through endurance.'

'Endurance?'

'All the chicks end up in harvesting before it's over.'

Panic took a hold of Victor, he'd already lost a wife and couldn't afford to lose Diana on this miserable stinking hole.

'Is there anything I can do?'

Sergeant Murray made a disparaging snort, 'Son, YOU'LL be lucky to make it, harvesting's gonna be backed up for a while.'

'I'll make it, and so will Diana.'

The Sergeant removed his cigar and shouted over the deck, 'OKAY ASSHOLES REPORT TO ASSEMBLY DECK C, YOU HAVE TEN MINUTES!'

On the way to Deck C Diana whispered, 'What were you discussing with Sergeant Murray?'

'Something about an endurance test. He said all women fail so we're going to stick together.'

'Maybe he was joking with you?'

'I don't think so … I have a bad feeling about this.'

A horde of corpses poured into Deck C creating orderly grey rows. Major Flatley waited upon his gantry, Sergeant Murray and his Marines below. A large pile caught Victor's eye, odd looking rifles, black combat suits of linen and layered flexible fibre reinforced vital areas. Large backpacks lay beside them, 'I guess we get our uniforms today,' whispered Diana.

Recruits awaited instructions, 'ATTENTION!'

The strident Major returned their salute, 'At ease recruits.'

He looked on with those dead eyes everyone possessed, he more so than any, 'For some, this is the end of basic training, for the few who succeed it may mark the beginning.

Today is endurance month, each recruit shall dress in full combat uniform, rifles are disabled but exact in weight and balance. Each recruit will carry a pack of fifty kilos, approximately half the weight of a large human male. You will be split into separate companies of twenty persons, navigating by yourselves, you shall be sent on timed marches through this vessel. Everything you need is inside your backpacks.

That was the good news, the bad news is you will be tested for four weeks whilst only being permitted to regenerate once a week.'

Immediately the Deck filled with concerned mumbles and chitter chatter.

'SHUT UP!' screamed the Sergeant; they stopped. Victor could inhale tension, closing in on all sides it tried to smother him with panic.

Major Flatley continued, 'Concern is warranted, after seventy two hours your body will begin to decay. Are there any questions before we begin?'

Diana raised her hand.

'Yes recruit?'

'How long can our bodies continue without regeneration, sir?'

'It's different for each person that being the purpose of endurance month, every Marine must complete this test before entering active service.'

He motioned toward a pile of combat armour, backpacks and disarmed rifles, 'You have thirty minutes to find yourself a weapon, uniform and backpack, I wish you all good fortune over the coming month,' the Major left through a side exit.

'YOU HEARD THE MAJOR, THIRTY MINUTES TO SUIT UP ASSHOLES!'

Worried looks were exchanged as men and women sorted burdens for the following month. Combat suits were very large in size, yet when filled by a recruit they contracted to fit comfortably. Combat boots worked in a similar manner, gripping the contours of a soldier's foot.

'Diana, make sure you get in my company, okay?'

'Sure.'

After twenty minutes Sergeant Murray's Marines split them into companies, RFID nanites alerted the ship's AI to the situation, now it would track them by company. Diana manoeuvred herself into Victor's company, grasping a heavy rifle whilst she gave half a fat guy a piggy back. The Private examined each man and woman then picked out Victor, 'You're leader of Echo Company, understood?'

He furrowed his brow.

'That means you'll be navigating the ship to your way point, understood?'

Victor tapped a device on the inside of his wrist pulling up a map of the ship, it disappeared, 'My map isn't working, sir.'

Private Morley nodded, 'You may only navigate to your way points via the provided hard map,' he gestured toward Victor's leg pocket.

Pulling out a piece of folded plastic it felt familiar, Victor knew he'd used something similar in a past life. Others met their maps with a confused expression but Victor's was one of familiarity, he identified their origin point before Morley.

'Excellent Mr ...'

'Zellmann, sir.'

'You're familiar with solid maps?'

'I don't know it just feels like I've done it before, sir.'

'Do you see your way points?'

'Here, here, here, until we come round to the regeneration hall, sir?'

'Excellent work Mr Zellmann, oh and you don't have to call me sir, I'm only a Private.'

'Yes sir, I mean Mr Morley?'

Morley smiled and nodded his head, 'I think you could go places Mr Zellmann ... if you survive,' he peered at Diana, 'is this your girlfriend?'

'Well I ...'

'Yeh I am actually,' snapped Diana.

'Good, emotional attachments provide incentive to keep going. You have twenty four hours to reach your first way point and check in, if you fail to do so a squad will recover your company for harvesting. If you reach it, any surplus time will be combined with the following twenty four hours given to reach the next way point and so on until on completion of the seventh way point you will arrive at Regeneration and recuperate for twenty four hours plus any extra time you may have accumulated, any questions?'

There was no reply.

Morley pointed toward an exit, 'Good luck recruits, see you in Regen!'

Victor marched forward holding a plastic map of S.S. Charon, waypoints clearly marked, nineteen members of his company followed.

'How far until the first waypoint?'

'About five kilometres.'

'Doesn't sound too bad.'

'You can manage with that pack?'

Diana tugged the straps a little, 'No problem.'

'Good, we should reach the first waypoint in an hour.'

Three hours later they arrived to discover a marker. Victor flicked a switch on its top informing S.S. Charon of their arrival. The Company opened backpacks whilst making themselves comfortable and dined upon nanite drinks, the dead didn't eat. Fifty kilos hanging on your back made the march far tougher than Victor first envisaged. Backs ached as they dropped packs to rest for a while. He measured distance to the following waypoint inside the engine rooms. He quickly realised it was ten kilometres and doubted they'd arrive in six hours. Looking forward he saw distance between each waypoint increased by five kilometres on the previous march.

'Damn, that felt like ten kilometres,' stated Diana as she slouched against a riveted wall.

Victor sucked a straw drawing fresh nanites to energize necrotic cells, 'Okay, let's rest for an hour then push on to the next waypoint.'

'What?' stated a member of Echo Company, 'we've got seven points and seven days; we'll be dead if we push that hard!'

'First off, you're dead already. Second the distance between each point increases by five kilometres each time, and I don't think anyone here can do a thirty five kilometre march in twenty four hours, certainly not carrying fifty kilos on their back.

So the only way we're gonna get to regen in seven days is if we push it from the get go, understood?'

A young lad snorted in response.

'You got a better idea kid?'

'I'll do what I want.'

'Fine, anyone that doesn't want a one way trip to harvesting can haul out with me in an hour.'

An hour later eighteen men and a single woman marched out carrying their burdens, one lad remained behind ... it was the last they ever saw of him.

Ten hours later, Victor's company reached their second point without incident. They collapsed into a heap as drinks were dug out of backpacks; a fellow took a swig then entered a nearby latrine, 'YEEEEAAAAAHHHHHH!'

His scream grabbed everyone's attention.

Victor slapped its door, 'Are you okay in there?'

A withering voice emanated from inside, 'My dick, oh Jesus, my dick!'

'What happened?'

The door opened, he staggered into the hall steam rising from his pants, 'I forgot about the piss.'

Some chuckled yet all realised the more they drank the sooner they'd have to urinate. Diana was concerned since it'd affect her ability to march more so, she didn't know how long she could keep it in but she'd have to let it out sooner or later, perhaps it was best to let a little out now rather than pay a higher price further down the road, she alleviated herself.

An hour later they marched on to the third point, fifteen hours of walking around hot engine decks, climbing up dark shafts and through tight air conditioning spaces was no fun, especially if your urinary canal burned like a Chinese firework factory.

Suction caps attached to hands and legs the team dragged themselves up a vertical shaft, 'Surely there's an easier way?'

'Trust me, if there were do you think I'd be doing this?'

'Vic, my arms cannot pull the weight.'

'Come on it's not much further, look I can see the maintenance vent.'

'No Vic, if I release my cup the backpack will pull me down.'

The rest of the company moved up toward a single light shining from an open horizontal tunnel. There was a scream, a recruit lost balance, he released a hand and knee suction cup at the same time despite instructions to move one at a time. Victor pulled his body against the shaft wall. Diana's burden prevented her from doing so. He released his left suction device. Distributing strain across his upper body Victor pushed Diana against the wall. The recruit flew past grazing them whilst desperately grabbing for something or someone. He disappeared out of sight, a faint thump echoed seconds later, they never saw him again.

Victor grabbed Diana's pack, pulling it off to wear opposite to his pack, now he had two burdens, one on his back and the other hanging off his chest, 'Can you climb now?'

She nodded her head in the darkness, 'But you cannot with two packs!'

'Take the rope out of my pack, climb up there and secure it inside, can you do that?'

'No problem,' she pulled a dark thick cord from Victor's backpack then climbed up into the open vent.

Five minutes later a looped cord descended to Victor's eye level. He put his arms through one at a time, securing his upper body inside, 'OKAY!'

Victor sensed a tug on the rope, as it alleviated his burden he climbed the wall one cup at a time. Suspended above an abyss the cord creaked under his strain, Victor was concerned every time he inched his load upwards until reaching safety where Echo Company recovered their leader.

From an operations room Major Flatley and Sergeant Murray observed Echo Company, 'His attachment to the girl forced him to use his brain.'

'You know they should've pulled the packs up then climbed it.'

Flatley nodded his head at a holo-screen as Victor climbed to safety, 'Mark him down I want to keep an eye on that one, Sergeant.'

'Yes sir.'

'Besides, Echo Company leads the pack despite a woman slowing them down.'

'She's tough, sir.'

'You know as well as I only seven women have ever made it into the ranks. Exceptionality will be the order of the day for this lady.'

'Maybe she'll get lucky, sir.'

'I didn't take you for a superstitious man, Sergeant.'

'Superstitious?'

'The number eight's considered lucky in the orient.'

Three waypoints and thirty five hours into the march Echo Company slouched around a pile of backpacks, nursing aches, wounds and fractures.

'One hour and we start for the next waypoint.'

His statement was met with groans.

'Yeh, I know it sucks but it's either this or harvesting.'

'Harvesting's looking better every time we hit a waypoint.'

'I'm not stopping anyone that wants their guts butchered; I'm giving the rest a chance for survival.'

A man in his late twenties scorned Victor, 'Survival? Dude, we're dead!'

'I'm not forcing you to do anything you don't want to, understood?'

'I guess if we all had a sweet girlfriend our feet wouldn't hurt so bad from blisters right now.'

'What's that supposed to mean?'

'Nothing,' he slouched down and took a swig of nanite drink.

'If you've got something to say, say it, we're all big boys here.'

'What I'm trying to say is there aren't exactly many females selected for the Marines and it's not like we get to socialize with the techs, engineers and pilots, so yeh some of us have motivational problems that maybe you don't quite understand ... unless you'll share some of her sweet ass with the rest of us?'

The corridor went silent, men got to their feet staring at Diana, fear lay in her eyes as desire smouldered within theirs. She was shocked that after thirty five hours of a punishing march they still had enough energy to even contemplate rape.

'Sit down kid,' stated Victor.

'There are thirteen of us and two of you, don't be stupid.'

Victor whispered, 'Diana, get your pack.'

'We just want to have a little fun, I mean come on she's dead, it's not like it's a crime or nothing.'

Victor and Diana moved backwards, facing a mob of young men who even in death remained slaves to their carnal desire. Victor clenched his rifle threatening to bash whoever entered range. Moving backwards they stepped past a bulkhead hatch, Victor dropped his weapon and swung the bulkhead shut, spinning a wheel until it locked.

'Come on, before they find a way around,' blurted Victor.

The pair rushed off hurriedly to thumps of frustration, her would be rapists had to navigate themselves now.

Victor and Diana forced themselves into a brisk pace to stay in front of their pursuers. Each time they reached a waypoint the marker switch hadn't been flicked, it was comforting to know they remained ahead in this game of cat and mouse. Not stopping to rest Victor and Diana marched on.

After exiting engineering decks the going was smoother, yet blisters ached and a stench of decaying flesh filled their nostrils. Victor felt himself become physically weaker, not due to fatigue or lack of sleep since the dead didn't require sleep. He sensed growing weakness as muscle tissue degraded, rotting like a corpse in the grave. Cold grey skin flaked away, eyesight blurred, joints stiffened and internal organs became less effective with every step. Victor had to breathe that much harder each passing kilometre.

Diana suffered the same grim disintegration, yet she had less tissue, smaller organs and so her burden weighed heavier. Pain from walking became horrific as bare burnt flesh rubbed, bone poked through her urinary tract. If it were not for Victor she'd have been raped and left for harvesting on the engineering decks. All the time she contemplated her near escape, had death made those men wicked or were they always such savage beasts? Yet Victor possessed not an evil bone in his body, perhaps that decade of experience between twenty and thirty years of age changed a man's character so radically he might begin as an amoral animal to end a principled human being? Or did he love her enough to risk his meagre existence for hers? She smiled at him and he smiled back galvanizing one another so they might ignore their hardships and march on.

The pair pushed hard during the first days so they might slow when decay set in, finally without any sleep, on the sixth day they arrived at regeneration to loud applause, the first in, they were immediately stripped, cleaned and set to rest inside regeneration units spending the following forty eight hours asleep while machines pumped nanites through their bodies repairing damage inflicted by the long march, preparing them for the following march. They'd come in twenty four hours early, providing valuable regen time, a crucial factor in the weeks ahead.

Chapter Four

Victor stumbled clutching an empty regeneration unit for balance, though his body had healed his mind remained diminished after a month of pressed marches. Taking a moment to recover he took note of something different, if not already dead it would've been chilling, more than half of units in this plush white hall of the undead lay empty. Their passports made out by the devil himself with a solitary visa stamped "Harvesting" in red ink on one of many blank pages. Inside Victor's mind Satan's mocking laugh bounced off the grim walls almost swallowing the bleak regular thud of his mark as it pressed upon their papers.

Diana rolled into reality, gathering herself before attempting to stand. He offered a hand lifting his love off the floor.

Another limp figure groped its way from a metal casket in a hall of morally beaten men, his short curly hair captured Victor's attention.

Victor stormed over and grabbed the fellow by his collar, 'You piece of shit!'

The young man recognising his assailant, 'Did the girl make it?'

'What's your name punk?' scanning a grey prison uniform Victor noticed his name patch sewn into the left breast, 'Michaels, just so you know you're a dead man!'

Michaels pushed back, 'Get your hands off me asshole!'

'WHAT THE FUCK ARE YOU TWO ASSHOLES DOING?' screamed Sergeant Murray.

'He attacked me and Diana during the long march, sir.'

Sergeant Murray's eyes narrowed on Michaels, 'Is that true son?'

'No sir! Zellmann and Zeng abandoned us somewhere in the engineering section, I was lucky to make it back, sir.'

Murray raised an eyebrow at Victor, 'Zellmann, is that true?'

'No sir, he and the remaining thirteen members of Echo Company attacked me and Diana.'

'You mean recruit Zeng?'

'Yes sir.'

'The trouble is Michaels is the only remaining member of Echo Company.'

'Then do a lie detector, sir.'

'Lie detectors are ineffective on the reanimated, dead men tell no tales.'

Michaels' smug expression further enraged Victor.

'OKAY ASSHOLES, DECK C IN 20 MINUTES, LAST ONE THERE'S ON LATRINE DUTY!'

Michaels swaggered away with two buddies, the only remaining member of Echo Company aside from Victor and Diana. After being "abandoned" then deciphering his map Michaels stumbled onto the regeneration deck just before time out.

Murray spoke under his breath to Victor, 'I shouldn't be telling you this but the Major reckons you might have what it takes.'

'I don't understand.'

'Just shut up and listen ... on arrival we deliver one to two hundred Marines to active duty. Out of that those Marines the Major has to provide Patterson with a Lieutenant a Sergeant and a Corporal, the rest are Privates.'

'Patterson?'

'Commodore Patterson commands the Necron.'

'I don't understand, sir.'

'What I'm trying to tell your dumb ass is that if you want to keep your girl safe you'd better make LT you knuckle head!'

'LT?'

'Lieutenant, make LT and Michaels is under your control, think about it.'

Victor nodded as he absorbed Sergeant Murray's wisdom.

'I've already said more than I should son.'

'Why are you helping me sir?'

'Because Michaels is an asshole, now get your ass on Deck before I have to kick it there son!'

'Yes sir,' Victor turned, grabbed a puzzled Diana by the hand and dragged her to assembly.

'What were you and the Sergeant talking about?'

'Nothing, I'm just looking after us.'

They entered the Deck and lined up in rows, Major Flatley walked onto his balcony.

'OFFICER ON THE DECK!'

Everyone stood to attention and saluted. Flatley resolutely stepped down and walked along rows of men examining those the long march had not consumed.

He stopped at Diana, 'What's your name recruit?'

'Diana, sir.'

'Do you have a last name Diana?'

'Zeng, sir.'

'You're the only female in this batch to complete the long march, you know what that means?'

'No sir.'

'It means you're one tough cookie. In all my time serving on the Charon do you know how many women I've seen complete the long march?'

'No sir.'

'Ten, including you recruit Zeng.'

Poised in a salute a wide grin emerged on her cold grey face.

'There are seven female Marines serving in Project Necron as we speak, do you think you've got what it takes to be number eight?'

'YES SIR!'

Major Flatley smiled at the short lady, 'That's what I like to see, a pair of balls on a woman,' his miserable demeanour resurfaced, 'You're gonna need them if you go up against the Drax.'

He moved onto Victor, 'Name?'

'Zellmann, Victor Zellmann, SIR!'

'You don't have to shout son, they gave me a new pair of eardrums ten years ago.'

'Sorry sir.'

'That was a joke son.'

'Sorry sir.'

Flatley glanced back at Diana, 'Does he always sound like a politician at confession?'

'Yes sir.'

Flatley nodded his head and continued down rows of recruits, 'Less than half of you remain, the rest have been harvested, any salvageable body parts and tissue, frozen, to be transferred aboard S.S. Necron along with those who pass stage five, you are now at stage three.'

He marched to the forefront where hundreds of automatic rifles lay on small foldaway desks, 'Today you will undergo weapons, special weapons and advanced combat skills training, good luck,' he returned the salute.

Flatley ascended his gantry and exited the deck.

The Sergeant stepped forward, 'EVERYONE TAKE A TABLE. STAND IN LINE WITH YOUR TABLE AND WEAPON IN FRONT OF YOU!'

Victor grabbed one of the many desks returning to where he stood, a large hologram lit up before the assembled recruits. A man began to dictate weapon safety and instruct on loading and disarming. The following hour was spent dismantling an N-13 automatic rifle. The N-13, a short weapon loading behind its trigger, ammunition came in the form of depleted uranium rounds. Its propellant a compressed inert gas, Nitrogen, loaded into the rifle butt.

The rifle was very basic, dismantling into five parts, Victor found it quite intuitive to disassemble then reassemble. A single clip held fifty rounds of standard ammo. Everyone passed the basic rifle test without problems.

Next came demolitions training, a wide variety of explosives both timed and triggered were demonstrated. From hand grenades to anti-tank mines to low yield nuclear devices, over the next three hours several men arrived in harvesting, unable to absorb information.

Victor became obsessed with passing and passing with flying colours, he had to get those pips or bars or whatever it was distinguishing him as an officer.

After weapons and explosives recruits moved on to aim and competency; a weapons range trundled in, they fired from their desks. Victor wanted to put a bullet in Michaels head, annihilating that smug antagonistic grin with a single pull of the trigger. Despite doing his best to ignore him he felt Michaels' eyes throughout the test, as if he knew something Victor didn't.

After an hour of practice recruits began testing on accuracy, rifles were compact and light yet kicked like a mule; it took some time to assimilate an aching shoulder, nevertheless he got a fix on the N-13.

Dropouts were wasted there and then before being hauled off to harvesting, due to the fact they wielded loaded weapons. Victor and Diana smiled nervously at each other through an uneasy atmosphere, nothing was certain.

'OKAY ASSHOLES PLACE YOUR WEAPONS DOWN.'

Rifles were returned to desks, collected by soldiers and replaced with small combat daggers. The blade was a slim diamond design, seven inches with a sharp point and two razor sharp edges. Its handle a ribbed vase design, well suited for Victor's grip. The entire weapon was constructed of high quality carbon steel.

Sergeant Murray pulled out his own dagger, 'Meet your new girlfriend recruits, her name is the Fairbairn-Sykes commando dagger, if you make it to active duty you will eat, sleep, breathe and shit with her by your side. She is your last defence, if all else fails you can rely on her to save your life.'

A young man folded his arms his face sent a message of disbelief, after rifles and explosives what good was a dinky little thing like that?

'You, is something wrong?'

'Well, what's a knife gonna do when the other guy's got a gun?'

The Sergeant motioned to Private Morley who exited the deck to return with a rifle, loaded magazine and propellant pack. He placed the items on a desk and returned behind the Sergeant.

'Come forward son.'

The young lad swaggered up until standing over the weapon.

'I'll tell you what son, if you can load that rifle and take me out, the Major will give you a free pass and what's more he'll make YOU a Sergeant.'

The fellow peered hesitantly at the rifle, mag and propellant pack.

'What's the matter son? I've got no firearm.'

More than ten seconds passed and nothing happened.

'You passed the time trail on weapon loading and firing today, less than three seconds, but still you ain't got the nuts to take on an old man fifteen metres away holding a knife. I'd say you answered your own question.'

The crowd chuckled ... the recruit snapped and lurched for the rifle, slapped in its propellant pack, reached for the ammo pack ... THUD, Sergeant Murray's combat dagger hit him square between the eyes. The recruit dropped to the floor unconscious, 'MORLEY, SEND HIM TO HARVESTING!'

'YES SIR!'

Two Marines dragged him to the exit. Murray yanked his combat dagger from the skull as it passed by, 'Do any more of you assholes doubt the Fairbairn-Sykes value?'

'NO SIR!'

He smiled, 'Then pick up your weapons and get a feel for your new best friend.'

For the remainder of the day recruits received instruction in basic knife combat skills, a few more visited harvesting. For the next month basic weapons and explosives training continued, becoming more advanced each day, dropouts piled up until a point was reached where so few recruits remained the cream had risen.

Victor and Diana spent another evening relaxing in the Enlisted Mess before regeneration. Michaels perched in the corner like an evil creature carved onto the side of a gothic church, mocking sinners and saints alike.

She plonked a bottle of vodka on the table alongside two glasses, 'Time to celebrate Vic.'

'What are we celebrating?'

She lifted her glass in a toast, 'To you of course.'

'Oh?'

'You came top in patrols and demolition numb nuts!'

He smiled, 'I forgot, sorry.'

'And for Christ's sake ...'

Victor cut in, 'Stop saying sorry!' they both laughed clinked glasses and knocked back libations.

She poured a second round of vodka, 'Since when were you such a swat?'

'I guess I'm either going into active duty or harvesting so screw it, why not try my best, and besides I've got kids on Earth relying on that Necron paycheque.'

'Uuuuurrrhhhh,' groaned Diana.

'Hey it's not like that, not anymore. I'm just saying.'

'Not wallowing in self-pity tonight?'

He smiled again, 'No we are definitely not, I'm sitting here with the most beautiful lady in this bar and I intend to screw her brains out before this evening comes to a close.'

'First I am the only lady in this bar; second I think you're being very presumptuous.'

'I guess I'll have to go into the latrine with some toilet paper like the other recruits,' he made a comical sad face.

'That's disgusting!'

'Not as disgusting as having a dump after twenty guys have been in there, imagine getting up and your back is stuck to the wall.'

'YUK! That's fucking gross!'

They laughed together yet the Mess failed to share the lovers' amusement, six months into basic training and only one woman survived, it was hard in more ways than one.

Victor consistently came top or amongst the top, he was pushing for the rank of 2nd Lieutenant. He didn't care about being an officer but the thought of Michaels making Lieutenant frightened him. Michaels was a competent recruit, he'd navigated himself back to regeneration during the long march and excelled in basic combat coming top in hand to hand and knife combat. The prospect of Michaels receiving 2nd Lieutenant and command over Diana motivated Victor more so than any distant memory of his family back home.

'I tell you what cowboy, why not start with a kiss and see what happens from there?'

They leant over the table meeting in a long smooch that captured every recruit's attention. Cold necrotic lips touched firing a shockwave of emotion in all directions, as if a stone had fallen into the middle of a lake sending out ripples. They relaxed into their seats, both sensed powerful aftershocks ricochet off grey walls.

In a cold dead and silent bar full of cold dead and silent men she whispered to Victor, 'Maybe we should go for a walk?'

'Sure.'

He took the bottle of vodka leaving hand in hand with the single surviving female much to the frustration of fellow recruits.

Strolling down Charon's corridors they arrived at an outer deck. Diana viewed stars burst into light, they twisted and warped in a struggle to keep up but only mankind had mastered the art of breaking Einstein's barrier, unless the Drax had also worked it out. She contemplated for a moment but they were far away, another four and a half years. Diana had only seen them on the NET and movies, they didn't seem so scary to her, being both taller and bigger only provided easier targets.

'Have you seen a Drax?'

'Sure,' replied Victor, 'There're loads on the NET.'

'What do you think of them?'

'Well they're damn ugly after you take the helmet off, reminds me of a bat.'

'Do you think it's true they attacked us first?'

'Who knows, we're in so deep, all that matters is who finishes it.'

They shared a swig of vodka.

'I heard people say U.S. carriers blockaded their home world and that's what started it.'

'Why the hell would they blockade the Drax?'

'The Drax home system is rich in Yeonum.'

'Are you sure?'

'You don't think they would have sent a whole carrier group to blockade them if their main export was broccoli!'

'Okay so assuming you're right, why the hell are they attacking our colonies?'

'All I know for sure is the 5th carrier group returned in a pretty sorry state and ever since we have been at war.'

'I remember that, they said the fleet was on patrol and got ambushed near Tau Ceti. Besides we don't know where their home world is so how could we possibly blockade it?'

'Sure because I believe everything my government tells me like a good little automaton.'

'I didn't take you for a conspiracy theorist.'

'So what's your theory? Drax appear out of nowhere and hit our colonies for no reason, making no demands, does that sound rational to you?'

'That's assuming they are rational, as far as I can see they're just animals.'

'Idiot! They learned to travel at near light speeds across the fucking galaxy of course they're rational!'

'So are you one of these Drax sympathisers?'

'I spent most of my life running from Triads, fighting to get my family out of poverty, I didn't have time to picnic on the Whitehouse lawn alongside middle class assholes with silver spoons in their butts.'

'Mouths.'

'What?'

'Born with a silver spoon in your mouth, not your butt.'

'Whatever! All I am saying is never underestimate your enemy Vic. If the Drax were just stupid animals this war would never of happened.'

'I guess you're right.'

'I am right, I've been fighting all my life and now I'm dead I have a new enemy, I don't plan on losing this time.'

He raised the vodka bottle, 'To the Drax!' took a swig and handed it to Diana.

She took the bottle, 'To the Drax?'

'Let's hope they are rational, because when they see Miss Zeng coming they'll retreat before a shot needs to be fired!'

She smiled and held the bottle up, 'To the most dangerous element in the galaxy … truth!'

He sighed out loud.

'Something wrong Vic?'

'You just made me think of something.'

'What's that?'

'In wartime the truth is so precious that she should always be attended by a bodyguard of lies.'

'Who said that?'

'Winston Churchill.'

'Who?'

'Come on Dee, the second world war?'

'Sorry, I went to a state school for the dispossessed.'

'So how come you know about this Sartre guy?'

'I found a book on an over-run military base, after the French pulled out. I taught myself to read and write French with it, turned out to be by Jean-Paul Sartre so I learnt philosophy at the same time,' she smiled at the memory. 'So what do you think Sartre would have to say about our predicament?'

Diana stared into nothing as cogs turned in her mind until she smiled again, 'We do not judge the people we love.'

Chapter Five

Twenty four hours of nanite mist flowed over the sides of his regeneration pod, rolling off its side as cold rain rolls down a window pane in winter time. Victor jumped out standing to attention for Sergeant Murray.

'First out again Zellmann, if you're trying to impress me it's working son.'

'Thank you, sir.'

Michaels popped up like one of those adverts on the internet that won't go away, you have to click fifty times before it disappears, then it's back in ten seconds ... some penis extension companies just won't take a hint. He stood to attention for the Sergeant somewhat dismayed Victor made it out before him.

'My two favourite boys always up before the herd.'

'Thankyou sir,' they replied in concert.

'You're gonna wish you stayed inside today.'

'What's up Sarge?'

'We're boarding and I ain't talking about surfing son.'

Diana pulled herself beyond swirling dreams of regeneration, abandoning horrors of past life on Earth inside a foggy unit to ascend as a beautiful angel of death into the afterlife and its own struggle aboard the Charon.

'Would you like to rest a little longer?' inquired the Drill Sergeant in a sardonic tone.

'Is that an offer Sarge?' replied Diana.

'GET YOUR ASS ONTO DECK B, NOW!'

Recruits flowed like water down a plughole, from regeneration and onto Deck B, a gargantuan area holding a small space vessel beside a tubular construction. Victor noticed the space vessel from news reels, a small patrol ship used by Drax.

Lining up in smart rows recruits waited before the gantry, a minute later its hatch opened, 'OFFICER ON THE DECK!'

Men and woman saluted as Flatley appeared to view his remaining candidates. Stood to attention between two spaceships, from two and a half thousand only two hundred hopefuls remained.

'At ease,' recruits stood arms behind and chins up, 'Today you begin boarding exercises, I expect half of you to be harvested before completion. Necron Industries funds this project for one purpose, can any of you knuckle heads tell me what that purpose is?'

A young man raised his hand.

'What's your name son?'

'Peterson, sir.'

'Okay, Peterson, what's the sole purpose of this project?'

'TO DEFEAT THE DRAX, SIR!'

Flatley shared a momentary smile with Sergeant Murray, 'Who told you that heap of shit son?'

Peterson exchange grey looks with fellow recruits, 'I just thought ...'

'Don't think son, that's what I'm paid for, anyone else?'

A sea of grey figures stood erect, as spines on a porcupine's back waiting for Flatley to solve his own riddle.

'Necron Industries is here to make a profit, nothing more, nothing less, boarding being the most vital skill required of a Marine. Necron Industries captures enemy vessels and claims salvage including new technologies, new technologies now available on Earth patented by Necron Industries.

So far this war has turned Necron Industries into the most profitable corporation in the history of mankind. We have shareholders all across the galactic arm, we are the only human corporation registered on the top five stock exchanges in the known galaxy, everybody knows the name Necron Industries and it all began with the discovery of a derelict alien ship fifty years ago.

Today we take vessels and their technology by force, despite the initial expense of Project Necron profit margins have exploded, this is the key to it all,' he pointed at vessels either side of the recruits, 'Military boarding and capture of an enemy vessel, there is no other species, no other military in the known universe which exceeds Necron in both ability and reputation when it comes to capturing enemy vessels, so good luck, I'll see half of you in six months.'

The Major exited through the same hatch, Sergeant Murray took the forefront, 'OKAY ASSHOLES GEAR UP!'

Victor walked forward to select a combat suit and a modified rifle, employing organic goo as ammunition rather than depleted uranium. Michaels bumped into him, 'Hey watch yourself Vic.'

'Only my friends call me Vic, and you're no friend of mine Michaels.'

Michaels had that smug look about him like the cat that got the cream, 'If you go to harvesting I'll be sure to look after your girlfriend's sweet ass.'

Victor took Michaels by the collar, 'Watch your mouth too.'

'What ya gonna do about it?'

'Maybe you'll catch a bullet in the back of your head Michaels, then they'll have to send YOU to harvesting.'

'YOU ASSHOLES GONNA SUIT UP OR LEARN TO DANCE?' screamed Murray. Fellow recruits laughed, Victor let Michaels go, 'Sorry sir.'

After two hours of technical training they split into teams for basic ship boarding tactics. Experienced Marines led each company of recruits and played the part of the Drax.

From one end of the deck remaining recruits watched on, cameras inside helmets allowed Sergeant Murray to point out useful tactics and mistakes. Recruits' helmets were black as the uniform; tubes along the side making its design seem more like an old gas mask. Each helmet's upper half was flat on the top, a pique hung over the face; from the occupant's point of view its carbon material was totally transparent.

Every man was ordered to turn his grav boots on, shortly afterwards gravity on Deck B was cut. Vessels floated toward one another, the tubular craft latched onto the thick square vessel with gravity hooks, Diana recalled suction pads she'd used to climb shafts during the long march.

Inside the boarding vessel Private Morley observed while two recruits used cutting tools to bore holes and insert explosive charges in a circular pattern. Once completed to Morley's satisfaction he ordered through his mic, 'TAKE COVER!'

They'd gone over this several times in theory, BANG, a distorted Drax outer hull containing circular tears remained. With one giant kick Morley knocked it in and entered the alien vessel, they boarded two at a time, a squad of twenty men, moving up to make room for the next two whilst covering the corridor at each end; The last man on board spoke into his mic, 'All aboard, sir.'

'Mercer and Ruiz you've got guard until we return, the rest of you follow me.'

Two men guarded a rough hole blown into the hull whilst ten moved in two by two formations leapfrogging one another around a corner towards the command centre, the other eight made double time toward engineering.

'I can't see a thing sir.'

'Use your night vision and the same for the rest of you, all Drax vessels look like this inside.'

Tranquil fog filled its corridors, an atmosphere most suited to the enemy, it made Victor think of the nanite mist inside his regeneration unit.

Unfortunately for Victor his vision was not suited to this gloomy, dank, fog. Despite a visual disadvantage he held an ace up his sleeve, many years ago it was discovered Drax depend predominantly on sonic waves to distinguish their outside world. To you and me that means they're not too hot in a noisy fire fight. As standard practice Marines would use the N-13's silencer, if caught in a firefight they had decoys, grenades which dispersed sonic waves to confuse the enemy, in other words a Drax stun grenade. Victor guessed that made him even but fighting in this alien environment still generated anxiety amongst recruits.

Morley pushed a fist into the air and everyone halted quickly taking defensive positions. Through the mist Victor saw nothing then switched to thermal, sure enough at the end of the corridor two men patrolled. Morley took aim and with two silent shots his targets felt an impact, game over boys.

A pair of recruits with goo splurged across helmets sat down whilst disabling their communications. Victor's team made their way to command.

Unguarded they burst in taking defensive positions behind workstations, yet no-one was there, they'd taken command. Victor let out a smile patting himself on the back until a shout went over his speakers, 'AMBUSH, HIGH!'

The Command Centre possessed another level where his enemy had taken up positions, a firefight ensued, Private Morley was taken out by green fluorescent goo along with four others.

'RETREAT, PULL BACK!' shouted Victor as he moved backwards returning fire on elevated ambushers.

After making it out of the Command Centre only three remained including Victor.

'Damn, we're fucked!'

'How many of them did you hit?' asked Victor.

'I think I hit one.'

'Smithy, what about you?'

'I saw nothing through that mist.'

'Okay time to fall back.'

The other two gave the thumbs up. Victor produced a sonic decoy, pulled the pin and tossed it into the mist before moving in the opposite direction. For the following five minutes it was a race to reach their vessel, trading goo with ghosts in the mist.

'Mercer, Ruiz, are you there?'

'Affirmative Vic.'

'Assault on Command Centre unsuccessful, seven down, we're on our way back, they're in close pursuit so don't hit us first.'

'Gotcha Vic.'

'Any word from Engineering?'

'Nothing.'

'Okay, we'll regroup at the entrance and work it out from there I guess, try to raise the engineering team, over and out.'

'Wilco Vic, over and out.'

Remaining Marines moved back firing into thick smog while comrades replied in kind. On arrival Mercer failed to raise those sent to dismantle engineering, Victor decided this was an unattainable situation, ending Murray's assessment by closing the hatch, releasing docking claws and floating away.

Gravity returned to the deck and men on both teams walked out, some covered in green goo, those defending received applause.

Sergeant Murray approached Morley, 'That was piss poor Private, taken by a standard Drax tactic like that, I expect more from you.'

Morley removed his gooey helmet, 'Yes sir.'

'I would expect more but this was a setup, Drax have predetermined ambush points on every ship, you assholes fell right into their trap.

In six months this and many other tactics will no longer prevent you from boarding and seizing a Drax vessel. Those who cannot adapt will be sent to harvesting, understood?'

'YES SIR!'

For the following six months recruits practiced boarding tactics over and over until it became instinct. Thanks to the exo-suit's extra sensitive sound and thermal detection recruits slowly transformed into warriors.

Many fell by the wayside. Major Flatley demanded the highest standards before a recruit might don the Necron Marine Corps black beret. Six months in, nearly one hundred recruits were culled. He was down to one hundred and twenty four recruits out of over two thousand. These men were tough enough to serve in any military, except Necron.

Flatley relaxed on an old sofa in his berth with his first officer, 'I hear your pilots are getting their wings soon.'

'Next month,' replied O'Brien.

They shared a bourbon and branch water, 'Bunch of arrogant faggots.'

The room was a direct reflection of Flatley's miserable attitude.

'You're not still holding a grudge?'

Flatley took a swig while staring into the cabin wall, 'Some bastard flyboy steals my wife and kids and I'm supposed to forget?'

'Jim, you were DEAD!'

'That skanky bitch still picks up a paycheque every month, I wasn't even cold and she was sucking off some hotshot yahoo ...'

'Jim, enough, I've spent two centuries on this ship and the story of your wife leaving your corpse for another man is wearing my nerves thin.'

Flatley sighed then activated a holo-projector, 'I want you to look at this,' an image from six months previous appeared. Victor's squad hit by an ambush during a boarding action, other images appeared of recruits in various situations where they assumed control, 'I have to pick and LT and I want you to do it for me.'

'I don't know anything about your troops, why don't you do it?'

'Because I've become emotionally attached, I can't make an objective decision.'

'I don't know,' he knocked back his drink, 'I pick my pilots, why the hell do I have to pick your Marine too.'

Flatley leaned over and filled O'Brien's glass, 'First off all your hotshots knew how to fly before they died. Second they all make LT so no hard decisions there.

I have to watch Marines fall by the thousand, none of them were special-forces before they died; it takes nearly three years for just one to make LT. That's a gamble I can't make objectively.'

'Okay, okay, it'd be a whole lot easier if Earth military hadn't blocked Necron.'

'The upside is we can instruct these bums for five years and still arrive at our destination a second after we left.'

'But we're not even eighteen months in yet.'

'I'm only looking at candidates right now, besides, I don't expect to lose more than a dozen or so recruits, they've got through the toughest part.'

'Don't believe it Jim, remember that time just one platoon made it? Jesus Christ the look on Patterson's face when only thirty recruits walked onto his deck, half the crew pissed their pants I'm sure of it!'

The two friends laughed at the memory, a particularly tough boot camp, the upside being a rich harvest.

'Next week and you'll be handing those pilots their wings.'

Flatley grimaced, 'You know what pisses me off most about that ceremony?'

O'Brien rolled his eyes, 'After two centuries of listening to you whine about it, let me think, no Jim I have absolutely no idea.'

'It's seeing those assholes walk into the officer's club like they own the fucking place, looking around for a fucking red carpet and reception committee. They all get LT and one of them gets Captain right off the bat, born at third base and thinks he hit a home run, the privileged class.'

'It looks like Bradley has picked a Chief Engineer.'

Flatley glanced from eternity to his first officer, 'Are you trying to change the subject?'

'I am.'

'When's the inauguration?'

'I don't know, he said it's a good crop … he meant the recruits.'

'Fine.'

The Commander sighed, 'Why don't I tell you another joke? That always cheers you up.'

'Go ahead.'

'Okay so Commodore Patterson he's being wheeled into surgery to have a circumcision, right?'

Flatley grinned, before sipping his bourbon.

'Well the surgeon comes out the operating room and walks up to the family and tells them he can't operate on him. The wife asks why and he says "I'm sorry but there's just no end to this prick!"'

Both men chuckled at the Commodore's expense … in another part of the vessel Victor and Diana sat in the Enlisted Mess drinking standard issue vodka, a pseudonym for rough as a bear's ass liquor.

'First in navigating and patrols, seems to me you are headed for the top.'

'Just keeping clear of harvesting.'

'Sometimes I wonder if it is worth it.'

Victor gave her a serious look, 'Hey, for sure it's worth it.'

She smiled, knowing someone on this ship cared about her was all Diana had to cling onto. Men and women falling like ears of corn in autumn led to many suicides. Grey skinned recruits casting themselves down shafts or shooting themselves through the mouth. Then there was the grimmest form of suicide, those who didn't have the nerve to do it themselves attacked armed guards or pretended to attack them with a deadly weapon … death by Marine. Many genuinely lost their minds, case after case of insanity filled the medical deck, a short stop on their way to harvesting.

'Do not worry Vic, I'm making the grade … do you know what's next?'

'No idea,' he played with his drink, 'but they can't push us any harder or there'll be no reinforcements left.'

'They must be a bunch of real hard asses. I hope we get into the same platoon.'

'That'd be nice.'

'I heard they promote three of us, one Corporal, one Sergeant and one Lieutenant.'

'Who told you that?' whispered Victor.

'I asked one of the Medics last week after he let slip Pilots were getting their wings.'

'Getting their wings what does that mean?'

'Uh, they all get Lieutenant and one gets Captain, can you believe it?'

'Damn, why didn't we get picked to be Pilots?'

'They all flew when they were alive. Only Marines have to do real basic training.'

Victor sneered as he took a slug of rough vodka, 'Bunch of assholes.'

Diana sniggered at his disdain

'What's so funny?' inquired Victor.

'You look like you swallowed a wasp.'

'Well they are a bunch of assholes.'

'You haven't even met one, besides I bet there are some really hot flyboys waiting to share a personal berth with a young naïve recruit like me.'

Victor's grey eyes opened wide, she sniggered again, 'Why Vic, I do believe you're jealous!'

'You're not funny,' he looked away towards the exit.

She got up and hugged him, a physically cold embrace yet her passion and his soul rubbed against one another creating warmth where none should exist, 'You want to walk?'

Victor protested her affections, 'I'm not in the mood.'

Diana placed her necrotic lips against his stone cold ear and whispered, 'I'll do that thing you like.'

Acting as a petulant child Victor folded his arms tighter, 'No thanks.'

'Okay, sorry about the joke, do you forgive me?'

'I guess so,' there was an awkward few seconds of silence, 'are you still up for doing that thing?'

She led him through the exit; the walking dead vanished inside an eternal night to enjoy each other's company, a moment of wild passion, hurtling through space beyond the speed of light.

Chapter Six

Nightmares taunted every moment of regeneration. Victor regurgitated a gravelly sludge infested with large maggots over and over. It took a second to pass the border of dreams into cold concrete reality. The taste of wet gravel hung on his tongue as he appeared from a metal coffin. Diana smiled, sprouting from her flower bed, in matching prison clothes. Michaels resembled a teenager hanging at the back of class, displaying a puerile grin.

Sergeant Murray puffed a cheap cigar, never seen without one on a morning, 'OKAY ASSHOLES, DECK C NOW!'

Recruits marched in an orderly fashion towards their destination; military discipline drummed into their heads over the past year. Lining up in rows one hundred and twenty four recruits stood at ease, six months of boarding tactics had ended in a final exam, many didn't pass.

Major Flatley stepped onto his parapet, 'OFFICER ON ...'

Before Sergeant Murray could finish every man and woman saluted the Major. Murray heard boots coming together and peered behind to take a look, 'the deck.'

'Good morning and congratulations on making it this far, you've spent more than a year training to be warriors but don't think you're finished. This is the Marine Corp not some holiday camp for pussy ass flyboys who made LT because they got pooped out the right birth canal!'

A chuckle passed over the recruits, the Sergeant let it slide, Flatley continued, 'Over the next six months you'll take instruction in combat survival, interrogation and resistance to interrogation techniques. Everyone I see here today should by all rights pass, but I know from experience there'll be dropouts. I'm not gonna say don't let me down, I'm not gonna say don't let your family down, I'm not even gonna say don't let yourselves down, what I AM gonna say is there are other Marines waiting for reinforcements and whatever is said on arrival they appreciate every man and woman who makes it into active service.

You'll be trained in basic torture techniques and how to resist standard Drax torture techniques, all those who pass will officially make Private,' he perceived an aura lift from his group of dead men and women, something like a child walking downstairs on Christmas day to find that present he or she whined for all year, 'ON PROBATION, that means your ass is still mine, if you fail to measure up at any time you will be harvested, that will be all,' he returned their salute and exited through a side hatch.

The next month was spent in lectures on escape and evasion techniques aboard Drax vessels followed by two months of practical testing. Theoretically they were going over the previous six months only far more advanced. Advanced weapons training included missile launchers, improvised traps, advanced man-to-man combat focusing on in depth knife fighting.

After completion another month of lectures began on resistance to interrogation and torture techniques, followed by two months of practical exercises culminating in a final exam.

Escorted to Deck B, where previously they'd practiced boarding over and over, a maze now filled its area. The insides of a Drax vessel had been counterfeited absorbing the entire space.

Combat suits rested in a pile, behind Sergeant Murray a group of men dressed in Drax uniforms awaited orders, deep blue, tubes reached behind from a hubcap on the chest connecting to a large triangular helmet. Much larger than a human helmet a sharp point protruded from its face, an evil omen of the beast's intentions. The party looked on in wonder; it was the first time they'd witnessed a Drax uniform in real life.

'This is what your enemy will look like on the battlefield, today's battlefield will be boarding actions.

This is the final exam you will be released without weaponry into a Drax transport.

My team will hunt you down over the next 48 hours, anyone captured will be interrogated for information. I don't expect everyone to evade capture and being captured is not an automatic fail since these men are Marines and you are not.

I do expect to witness what you've been taught over the last six months, you are only to give your name, rank, serial number and date of birth. All other questions are to be answered how?'

As one recruits shouted, 'I CANNOT ANSWER THAT QUESTION!'

'Excellent, NOW SUIT UP!'

Combat suits shrunk to fit recruits perfectly, helmets clicked into place its seal fixed tightly around their suits neck brace.

Everyone lined up ready to go, a large pair of cargo doors opened inviting recruits inside, 'You have twenty minutes before the hunt begins, good luck, NOW GET YOUR ASSES MOVING!'

Victor and Diana entered side by side, it need not be said but they remained together. Victor pointed toward what he believed to be the engineering section, a well ventilated area possessing plenty of tight crawl spaces. Murray's team would have difficulty negotiating such cramped areas in those big monster suits.

Changing their suits to match frequencies they spoke, 'Forty eight hours, you think we can do this Vic?'

'Sure, crawl spaces are too tight in the cooling vents.'

Somewhere else on the ship searching for a medical crate to hide inside, Michaels scanned frequencies. Victor's nemesis finally tuned in picking up Victor and Diana, his sinister grin widened. He listened in on their conversation as they ran through swirling mist. He searched a nearby compartment and found a container of large thick syringes no doubt used for treating Drax in an emergency. Michaels took one, placed it in a leg pocket and with that devilish grin cautiously made his way out of the medical section, shuffling off to engineering.

Marines in Drax uniforms moved inside the vessel armed with live weapons, it was time to put recruits to the test.

Twelve hours later Diana and Victor lay in a ventilation pipe waiting out the timer, 'I hope they don't check these vents, there's no way to escape.'

'What are they going to do even if they check the vent?'

'They could rip it open, did you ever think of that?'

Victor sighed, 'Do you have a better plan?'

'We could use the water tanks, hide in them.'

'There's one problem with that plan, they're already full of water.'

'How do you know?'

'Oh come on Dee there's no way Murray would make a dumb mistake like that, which tells me if they aren't full it's a trap.'

She shrugged, 'Just a suggestion.'

Thick fog swept over their bodies flowing as wine dark waters of the Styx. Its eerie silence made Diana uncomfortable, she didn't like cramped spaces … not that Victor did.

'Still it might be worth checking out.'

'And if they're full what happens when we get inside Archimedes?'

She thought for a short time and realised he was right, the water would have to go somewhere other than the tank leaving clear evidence for Murray's hunters. Diana groaned, 'Uuurrrhhh, you're such an annoying little swat you know that?'

'Stop, did you hear that?'

'Hear what?'

'I'm sure I heard something,' a faint noise excited Victor's speakers, was it the flow of dark smog or someone breathing, he was unsure and uncertainty made architects nervous. In their pitch black pipe a lesser person would have lost control to the Sons of Ares … terror and panic. Victor held it together not because he was tough but because he'd protect Diana at any cost, that and the fact she'd never let him forget it if he cracked, 'I think someone's listening.'

The pair remained silent, listening for the slightest squeak, viscous mist poured over their bodies as torrents over rocks in a river bed, only the clank of machinery could be detected.

'You're paranoid.'

'Sometimes the paranoid are being hunted by crazy men in big blue monster suits!'

His shoulders were pushed together, movement a painful task up here in a duct too small for any Drax and not very accommodating for the average human.

Diana observed a timer projected on her helmet glass, she sighed, 'Only thirty six hours to go.'

'Shhhhh, I'm sure someone's listening, cut the banter.'

'Yes sir,' replied Diana in a sardonic Chinese accent, 'Your boots need shiny shiny sir?'

'Give it rest I'm only …'

'Having fun kids?' said Michaels giggling like a buffoon over their speakers.

'Go fuck yourself asshole,' snapped Diana.

'Shhhh, don't reply, he could be collaborating with the enemy.'

'No, no, definitely no, I am not collaborating, never not in a hundred years.'

'Got tired of listening to your own bullshit? Well join the club Michaels everyone's sick of your weird ass!'

'Shhhh, don't communicate with him again, understood?'

'I don't take orders from you Vic.'

'You tell him Dee!'

'When we get outta here I am gonna rip your tiny pencil dick off and send it to harvesting, maybe someone needs a new nose hair!'

'Can't we be friends Dee?'

'You're not my friend asshole.'

'Will you do that special thing for me Dee?'

'I'M GONNA FUCKING KILL YOU WHEN I GET OUTTA HERE!'

'SHUT UP,' shouted Victor.

'DON'T TELL ME TO SHUT UP, I'M NOT YOUR SLAVE!'

Michaels cackled through thick fog, 'I need something special little Dee.'

'HOW'S A BULLET IN THE HEAD SOUND!'

A long thick syringe needle burst through the thin vent floor and into Victor's leg piercing his suit, 'JESUS CHRIST!'

'He says hi Vic,' giggled Michaels.

Another thud hit their underneath, Victor took a second hit to the body, thick red fluid began to seep out until his suit contracted, covering his wounds.

'Maybe we do need to get out of here,' said Victor as they scrambled to drop out the vent while a madman punctured its floor, if his helmet glass were ruptured he was going to harvesting.

Victor and Diana jumped down, Michaels turned on the lights inside his helmet, a menacing visage of evil sneered through dense mist. Perhaps he was trying to terrorize them? If so it was working.

Pointing a Drax syringe he laughed in an uncontrollable manner, 'First I'm gonna send you to harvesting, then I'm gonna have some fun with my little Dee.'

Victor moved forward to fight, Diana held him back, 'You're injured, you can't fight.'

Michaels was top of the class in hand-to-hand and knife combat, she was certain Victor couldn't win.

'Get out of here Dee,' said Victor.

'Vic stop being an asshole,' replied Dee.

'I said get out of here.'

'I don't take orders from you Vic. I'm not your slave!'

'He'll kill us both!'

Michaels cackled, 'I just want to kill YOU Vic, I have special plans for little Dee, special plans,' he fondled his crotch in the most revolting manner. Michaels paused for a moment, peered over their shoulders then disappeared into the Drax mist as quickly as he had come upon them.

They turned to thank their saviours only to witness Drax hunters with weapons aimed, a strange alien click lit their chest hubcaps before a translation pumped through in a deep voice, 'On your knees, hands in the air human!'

Diana turned to Victor as she knelt, 'Great plan Vic.'

'Why's it always my fault?'

'Because you always apologise for it.'

'Sorry.'

'UUrrrhhh!' Diana received a boot in the gut from a hunter.

Victor was led at gunpoint into a small grey room. Captors' rifle barrels directed him to a large reclined seat, he sat down, thick braces made from a cord fibre shot across his chest securing him in place.

The door closed, shortly afterwards the Drax mist dissipated. One of the captors removed Victor's helmet preventing any communications beyond their parlour.

One of the captors made a high clicking noise, his hubcap lit up in odd patterns, a translation pumped into the cell, 'Who are you?'

'I am Recruit Victor Zellmann, serial number 02672, date of birth September the 19th 2660.'

Another alien ticking noise along filled his ears, 'Why are you here?'

'I cannot answer that question.'

'Why?'

'I cannot answer that question.'

'What can you answer?'

'I am Recruit Victor Zellmann, serial number 02672, date of birth September the 19th 2660.'

His captor nodded toward the other, it pressed a long finger on its wrist and pain ran through Victor's body, nerve centres lit up like a Christmas tree. For the next hours (he didn't know how long exactly) Victor was tortured, no questions, no pomp and circumstance, no crazy guy stroking a Siamese cat like in the movies, just horrific pain, his captors' device excited selected nerve centres depending on their perverse whims.

Lights faded to black, he couldn't see or hear anything, deaf to even his own screams the hell continued. Pain focused on an area until it lost its edge, suddenly a different part of his anatomy began to scream out as witches burning at the stake, shrieking to the sky for deliverance as the flames of hell lick higher and higher. He howled in misery yet neither heard nor saw anything which somehow intensified his suffering.

Lights returned, gradually revealing his tormentors. The fact they'd remained in the same position during his torture served to unbalance his mind, 'Who is your commanding officer?'

That gruff alien voice was a relief, 'I am Recruit Victor Zellmann, serial number 02672, date of birth September the 19th 2660.'

Light and sound off, pain centres ignited, his torturers silently observed … this was going to be a long night.

Hours later his miserable cell illuminated, his body cramped with pain, nerves ready to detonate on the smallest movement, he tried to sit still but something always decided it was time, an itch, breathing in and out, the mere act of moving his eyeballs and their lids sent a shock of pain through his brain, which by now felt like a traumatised jellyfish on Centauri crack.

'Who is your commanding officer?'

'I am Recruit Victor Zellmann, serial number 02672, date of birth September the 19th 2660.'

A hologram appeared on the wall, it was Diana, beautiful Diana, screaming as pain coursed her body. Tears ran a trail down her face, straps secured her body in an embrace of torment, jolts of agony shook her to and fro.

'Answer my question, who is your commanding officer?'

'I am Recruit Victor Zellmann, serial number 02672, date of birth September the 19th 2660,' he waited for the inevitable response but it didn't come. Instead Diana's lower half was stripped naked, each leg braced by fibre straps and pulled apart. An interrogator pulled out a rifle and moved toward Diana, who watched on in fear, her expression of dread and isolation struck him beyond any physical torture. For it was now Victor understood the truth of his relationship with Diana Zeng, any man or beast that might commit such evil acts upon her would hurt him more than had it murdered him. Victor realised he could not be physically tortured into compliance but through her they could make him the most wretched being in the universe.

'Tell me who your commanding officer is or he fucks her ass.'

'I am Recruit Victor Zellmann, serial number 02672, date of birth September the 19th 2660,' he didn't believe they'd actually do it ... he was wrong. Victor tried to push through his binds, to no avail, he was stuck watching a bunch of creeps violate Diana. She cried, her denigration another tactic, unknown to Victor they all would suffer it. For later she observed him take a rifle barrel from behind, feeding a puddle of thick nanite blood below. The images were false, created by Charon's computers yet impossible to distinguish from reality. Victor held on, he trusted Diana, he had faith she would pull through and they be reunited in a day.

Once the examination was over recruits who had avoided capture walked out, Michaels being one of them. The rest were carried into regeneration, unconscious, those who failed had already taken a one way ticket to harvesting hours earlier.

Forty eight hours later Victor awoke from his dreams to a feeling of great joy, beautiful Diana was alive, so to speak. They embraced one another, 'Nice to see you Private Zellmann.'

His greatest concern had been for her all along, the fact he'd made it into active duty, if only technically, was of no consequence. Still it made him stop and think for a moment, he was finally a Marine … on probation.

She smiled and looked up at his face, 'What is it?'

'I forgot we made it in.'

'What else were you thinking of Vic?'

He stared into her eyes, beautiful auburn trying to escape a grey sheen of death. Victor squeezed her waist, slender and eloquent as that of a butterfly. After a long kiss she smirked, 'It seems there is something more important than making LT.'

He peered over her head to see their regeneration units laying side by side, one read "Zellmann, Victor" penned on a piece of plastic above "Serial Number: 02672" embossed into the booth's metallic frame. On the next unit he read "Zeng, Diana" on a plastic sticker above "Serial Number: 02673" firmly fabricated onto the frame of her unit.

Zeng and Zellmann, their family names brought them together, placing them side by side in the two final regeneration units. Thanks to that fact the first human he met after death was Diana Zeng, a beautiful orchid vibrant with colour in a field of withered and dead weeds.

Trapped on a cursed ship of the dead she was all he had left to hold onto, he cared not for family on Earth they were distant memories he could not recall during daytime and during night haunted rather than comforted. Victor had stumbled across someone to love and if lady fortune permitted, might love him, he would fight to keep her.

Chapter Seven

Of men and women resurrected from tombs of cold metal nearly two years ago ninety three remain today. Old two piece jump suits familiar to a communist work camp replaced by uniforms of S.S. Necron Marines.

Recruits burst with pride, adorned in combat fatigues. Skull and crossed rifles fashioned from white gold glinted in the light.

Major Flatley appeared on his gallery with O'Brien, recruits saluted their commanding officer. The pair strolled down to the floor of Deck A, a surprising amount were lost during resistance to interrogation, more than thirty men. Flatley consoled himself with the fact he'd produced thinner crops than this.

His boot touched the Deck, a masquerade ball of grey smiles ignited warmth inside, these moments kept him going. After returning salutes and silently examining every single Marine Flatley stood beside Sergeant Murray and Commander O'Brien, 'Well done Marines, in three years I hope to deliver you all to the S.S. Necron, once there I expect you to honour your fellow Marines who've worked so hard instructing you.'

Flatley gestured toward O'Brien, 'This is Commander O'Brien, he looks after the engineers, technicians, medics, flyboys and anyone else born on third base!'

A ripple of laughter reverberated around Deck A, the commanding officers let it slide, 'As you may know basic training and selection ended for Commander O'Brien's boys more than a year ago, if you were the Chief Engineer of a star ship before death your past abilities will return thanks to enhanced revival technology, kinda like riding a bike.

None of you went through this process since Earth military blocked personnel from signing contracts with Necron, they want body parts for themselves, added to that they hope to discover Necron's unique revival technology. So every Marine has to learn to be a Marine from scratch and not just any Marine but a Special Forces Commando ready to fight and win the moment his boots hit the deck.'

The Major motioned to the Commander who passed over a small wooden box. He opened it, 'Now I know you've heard rumours that three of you will be selected for promotion, that's true.'

Marines waited with bated breath, they'd been gossiping about this for years and now it was here. Michaels' evil smirk leered at Diana, Victor locked eyes with Michaels and despite his cold defiant stare Michaels continued to grin like a demon.

'EYES FORWARD!' bellowed the Sergeant.

They looked forward as Flatley continued, 'There will be three promotions before we reach the Necron, first of all Private Mercer, front and centre.'

Mercer stepped out of from the pack.

'Come here Private Mercer.'

He marched forward, Flatley proceeded to pin two sets of Lovats onto his shoulder straps. The double stripes of a Corporal fashioned from white gold gleamed on his uniform.

'For your outstanding performance directing heavy weapons, you are promoted to Corporal, well done Corporal Mercer,' he handed Mercer the box, 'you may return to your previous station.'

Mercer saluted, Flatley replied and the lad took his place in line.

Another wooden box was handed to the Major, 'Private Michaels front and centre.'

Michaels stepped forward.

'Come here Private Michaels.'

Victor's worst fears had become reality, yet one last shot remained to keep Diana safe.

Flatley opened the box, took out a pair of white gold Lovats, three stripes, 'For your outstanding performance in hand to hand, knife combat and terror tactics you are promoted you to the rank of Sergeant third class,' Flatley pinned the white gold on his shoulders and passed Michaels his box, 'well done Sergeant Michaels.'

Michaels saluted, Flatley returned it, 'You may return to your previous station.'

As Michaels mingled he fired a smirked across Victor's bows, Victor wanted to punch that guy in the face so bad but all he could do was hope to make LT, if not he'd frag him at the first opportunity.

'Zellmann, front and centre,' Victor snapped out his malaise of hatred and Michaels lost his signature giggling fool visage.

Victor stepped forward, heart beating like a bass drum.

'Come here Private Zellmann.'

He marched over, yet from Victor's perspective he floated in a dream state, others served as minor characters in an opera watching on as its hero ended the final act in a dramatic crescendo, it reminded him of an ancient quote, "The best revenge is success" or maybe it was from the atomic era? He couldn't remember but whoever said it was right. The Major and Commander peered back through a haze; finally it cleared as he came to a stop.

Opening the box Major Flatley pinned a white gold star on each shoulder strap, 'For your outstanding performance in patrols, direction of artillery, air support and leadership you are promoted to the rank of 2nd Lieutenant, well done 2nd Lieutenant Zellmann,' Flatley offered the box though it took a few seconds for Victor to reach out and accept, afraid it might cause the curtain to fall and break his perfect fantasy.

'What's the matter son?' whispered Flatley.

'Nothing, nothing sir,' Victor accepted the box, this was no fantasy, the Major was still there looking into his eyes.

'You may return to your station Lieutenant Zellmann.'

Victor walked back eyes fixed on Michaels, relishing every moment of his nemesis' despair.

Major Flatley surveyed his Marines, 'There will be a further year of training in various tactics concerning underwater demolitions, reconnaissance, beachhead assault and warfare on multiple planetary environments.

After that you will graduate then continue training until we reach the Necron. You are all Marines, you are the best ... remember that.'

The officers returned to their gantry and exited the Deck, every Marine saluted until they'd gone.

'AT EASE,' Sergeant Murray puffed his cheap cigar, 'Okay you've got one week rest and recuperation before planetary tactics begin, dismissed.'

Diana ran straight up to Victor, 'Congratulations!'

'I guess I get to order you around now.'

She went on her tip toes and whispered in his ear, 'Not if you want the special thing.'

Victor laughed as comrades shook his hand in congratulation, except Michaels, he was bitter as winter in a Russian gulag. No longer did he grin like an idiot, rather he sneered in disdain, hatred boiling to the brim of his pitiful soul, opportunity stolen by cruel fate, at least that's how he saw it.

Sergeant Murray approached Victor and saluted, 'Congratulations Lieutenant.'

It was a odd feeling to say the least. Rather than screaming orders down his ear Sergeant Murray saluted in a calm tone.

'May I escort you to your cabin, sir.'

'I have a cabin?'

'Yes sir, all officers have a cabin, sir.'

'Thankyou Sergeant I'll get my things first.'

'Your effects have already been moved to your cabin, sir.'

Well he only possessed a second pair of fatigues at the moment and a mess uniform so he took Diana along to inspect his new digs, 'Please lead the way Sergeant.'

They marched onto an upper regeneration deck, through corridors never seen by Marine recruits up until now. He felt like a galley slave that had been released from his irons to serve above deck with the gentry, plaques decorated cabin doors, 'Who are they Sergeant?'

'Mostly pilots, sir.'

'Why so many?'

'Every pilot makes LT, sir.'

'Why?'

'Only officers are permitted to pilot spacecraft, sir.'

They reached a metal hatch with his name embossed on a plaque, 'Here we are sir.'

Murray stood to attention and saluted again, 'Congratulations sir.'

'Dismissed Sergeant,' he returned the salute and Murray marched back down the corridor.

Victor stepped inside his cabin, it contained a bunk, a regeneration booth, a latrine and a shower with basin and mirror. Victor opened his locker, much larger than an enlisted man's. Inside hung uniforms, combat, mess and dress uniform which included a sabre in a golden sheathe.

'Damn, I guess it won't take long to forget about me.'

'Dee, I'm not going to forget about you, trust me.'

'Promise?'

'I promise, hey will you be my date to the officers club?'

'But enlisted aren't allowed in there.'

'I'll swing it somehow, is it a date?'

'Sure, do I have to wear a dress?'

'Mess uniform will do.'

Diana smiled, 'When?'

'1900 hours okay for you?'

'Sure.'

'I'll come and pick you up, where'll you be?'

'Waiting in the Mess,' she stepped outside, 'see you then!'

Diana hadn't got far down the hallway when an officer stopped her, 'Private what are you doing here?'

She stood to attention, 'I was accompanying the Lieutenant, sir.'

'I don't see a Lieutenant, Private.'

'Lieutenant Zellmann, sir.'

'I'm not aware of a Lieutenant Zellmann, Private.'

'He was just promoted, Sir.'

'Just promoted, no-one was promoted today ... in fact no-one has been promoted for over a year now.'

'He is a Marine, sir.'

The pilot's eyes narrowed, a man in jet black with white gold adorning his beret and shoulders stepped out of a cabin, 'She's accompanying me Lieutenant.'

The pilot was dressed in his beige uniform, blue beret, a cap lovat fashioned from twenty two karat gold into a pair of wings spread out behind a skull wearing a beret, his shoulders sported single golden stars, 'Enlisted aren't permitted on this deck … unless on latrine duty, are you on latrine duty Private?'

'I said she's accompanying me Lieutenant, let it go.'

He growled before returning to his cabin, the door closed, its plaque read, "2nd Lieutenant Eric Clarke".

'What an asshole!' declared Diana, officers in the hallway stopped and stared at the young girl.

'Flyboys what can I say?' Victor escorted Diana to the elevator where she waved goodbye. Somehow he was going to have to swing this date tonight, his wrist device began vibrating. Victor pulled back his sleeve, a request to attend the Major's cabin in twenty minutes.

Dressed in Mess uniform Victor made his way to the upmost floor on the regeneration deck and walked down a tight corridor ending with two armed Marines guarding a hatch. On the hatch a plaque embossed with the words "Major James Flatley" rested at eye level.

'Lieutenant Victor Zellmann.'

One of the Marines whispered. A mic woven inside his shirt collar picked it up, 'Lieutenant Victor Zellmann to see you, sir.'

'Let him in.'

The Private slung his rifle back and spun the lock, opening the hatch then closing it behind him.

Victor stepped in to see a comfortable room of old leather and mahogany, a writing desk with a window into space, a bed with a regeneration unit above it and an old sofa which seemed out of place in the Major's cabin.

Major Flatley rested on the sofa with Commander O'Brien, both of them drank a coloured liquor he suspected to be whisky. Victor saluted, 'At ease Lieutenant,' he stood with legs slightly astride and arms behind his back, 'I said at ease, you look constipated son.'

O'Brien and Flatley sniggered as they sipped drinks, both slightly inebriated. Victor brought his arms to his side standing as loosely as his uniform permitted.

'I wanted to congratulate you personally, drink?'

He was curious to try the liquor, 'Thank you sir.'

'Take a seat,' Flatley gestured toward a wooden chair as he poured from the bottle.

Victor brought the glass to his nose and took a sniff; it reminded him of bourbon, tasting confirmed its nature, a nice change after two years of vodka akin to rocket fuel made obsolete by Yeonum reactors.

'I always have a drink with my Marines,' he opened a box of cigars, 'smoke?'

Victor looked inside tentatively, his wife had banned any form of tobacco since the children, 'I don't smoke, sir.'

Flatley and O'Brien took one each, 'Don't worry son, it's not going to damage your health,' they both laughed.

'You know why I have a drink and a smoke with my Marines?' he clipped and lit his cigar with a table lighter.

'No sir.'

'I was a Marine, Special Forces.'

'I thought ...'

'Military put the block on Necron, heh, a few got through the net first. Me for one,' he motioned with his glass at O'Brien, 'John and when you get aboard the Necron Colonel Clifton Rockey and Commodore Ranulph Patterson.

Now me and Cliff were both Marines, Special Forces, so we know what it takes and we respect that, but you're gonna run into a lot of assholes that got an easy road into the service.'

'I think I met one today, sir.'

Flatley smirked, 'Especially all these hotshot pilots.'

O'Brien fell back into the old couch, 'Not again Jim.'

'You see Commander O'Brien was one of those hotshot pilots that walked into a bar in his Space Force uniform specifically designed to turn normally rational women into wild ovulating animals.'

O'Brien shook his head, Victor had to chuckle along with Flatley's narrative, 'Your average Space Force pilot spends six months learning not to crash his ship into the side of a carrier ... in a simulator, gets an officer's uniform and spends the next six months being treated for Epsilon syphilis!

You spend years going through a selection process staring death in the face every day and I'm proud of every one of you,' he raised his glass, 'to the Marines.'

After having a sip Victor spoke, 'I would like to make a request, sir.'

'This one doesn't wait around Jim!' stated O'Brien.

'What is it son?'

'I'd like to bring a date to the officers club tonight.'

'You have my blessing Lieutenant.'

'You didn't ask who, sir.'

'Private Zeng, right?'

'Yes sir.'

'You're close to her, aren't you.'

'Yes sir.'

'Don't get too close.'

After finishing his drink Victor was excused, O'Brien sighed, 'I do believe he's in love Jim.'

Flatley took another slug and rolled his lips back as the spirit went down, 'Lucky bastard.'

'I still say you should've promoted Michaels.'

'Guys like Michaels attract bullets and I'm not talking about enemy fire.'

'Yeh but promoting a guy who's obviously in love with one of his Privates, that can't be good.'

Flatley gazed stoically at his cabin wall, 'At least he gets to experience love again, for the rest of us it's just fucking corpses in the hope one day we rise from our tomb minus a little emptiness.'

'I stopped looking for love long ago.'

'I know.'

'Well good luck to Lieutenant Zellmann and Private Zeng.'

'Here, here,' they clinked glasses in a toast knocking down some more bourbon, Flatley looked at his wrist, 'we've gotta get ready.'

'What for?'

'He's taking Zeng to the officers club tonight.'

O'Brien grimaced at his friend, 'You're a dirty bastard you know that?'

'This'll be the high point of my journey, watching some of your pussy ass flyboys get bitch slapped by a Chinese girl half their size.'

'And you get to massage that centuries old chip on your shoulder.'

'And your glory boys learn an important lesson,' he pointed at O'Brien who sighed in defeat, 'Don't fuck with the Marines.'

Chapter Eight

Marines clapped and cheered as Victor entered the Mess in his officer's uniform, he cut quite a dashing figure. Black with scarlet lines, his peaked cap displayed the venerated Necron Marines emblem in white gold, a pair of shiny shoes reflected the ceiling lights.

Diana was dressed in tunic and trousers of the same colours, as an enlisted Marine she wore a beret. Happiness welled up inside contrary to death's grim barrier, he kissed her fingers splitting love's atom so all might view its white light.

'May I have the pleasure of escorting you tonight?'

'You may.'

He crooked his right arm, Diana threaded hers to cheers, all except Michaels he refused to let it go, 'Nice uniform, did your mother make it for band practice!'

The room fell silent, on revival such antics might have been amusing, yet today an officer was no longer sport for mockery.

Victor stopped to face his devilish nemesis, 'Did you say something Sergeant?'

An aura of anxiety cloaked the room.

'I was just commenting on your uniform.'

'GET UP SERGEANT!'

Michaels slouched on a bench beer bottle in hand, 'Fuck you.'

Everyone had been expecting this for nearly a year and it seemed the time had arrived. Victor pulled back his tunic sleeve, tapped his wrist, 'Report to Deck twelve, section five, that's an order Sergeant.'

'I said stick it up your ass.'

Victor called over his shoulder, 'Corporal Mercer and Private Morley, escort Sergeant Michaels to Deck twelve, Section five, make certain he's secured properly.'

'Yes sir!' Michaels hand hovered above his combat dagger, 'Don't do this,' whispered Mercer. For a few seconds everything was up in the air, no-one sure of what the other intended or how far they were prepared to go, 'You'll go to harvesting,' stated Morley.

Michaels stood up, tossed his beer bottle on the floor and saluted in the most acrimonious manner. Victor returned the salute, Michaels was escorted to the brig.

Michaels exited to spend an evening in the brig whilst Victor accompanied Diana to the officers club.

The pair walked through upper decks arm in arm turning heads amongst flyboys and Techs, 'If you think Michaels was a dick before you should see him now,' stated the young lady.

'I guess those extra stripes have turned the ships' asshole into a black hole, if you get my meaning.'

'Yeh but it's nothing to do with stripes on his arm, it's about stars on your shoulder Vic.'

'Why?'

'First you got the girl,' she squeezed his arm tight, 'then you got LT, that asshole is out to get you. My advice, do not turn your back on Michaels not even for a second especially when weapons are loaded.'

'Has there been any talk?'

'He's talked or should I say whined about nothing else.'

'What do the others say?'

'Michaels is obviously insane but he made Sergeant what's a Private supposed do?'

Victor nodded, 'We'll see about that.'

Strolling corridors they heard chitter chatter, on turning a corner it pointed to the officers club. Victor and Diana smiled at one another before he led her inside. Much like any Mess there was a bar with drinks, yet here drinks possessed greater range and class, billiard tables were present, something neither of them had witnessed since arriving on the Charon, solid food, its smell was alien yet excited memories of the past. Victor inhaled the aroma of hotdogs, mustard and fries, it took him back to living in New York where he worked on building projects, he'd often go outside to grab a quick meal.

Their jackets and caps were taken by a concierge, Victor didn't even realise due to the exotic flavours he attempted to identify.

They were held in awe for a moment, suddenly broken by some six foot six, blonde haired red neck, 'Hey man, this is the officers club, no enlisted.'

Victor came out of his trance and looked up at the 2nd Lieutenant, obviously a pilot due to his slick uniform, 'She's my date for tonight Lieutenant.'

'I don't care if she's the Virgin Mary, I don't drink with enlisted,' he looked down his nose at Diana as if she were unfit to breathe the same oxygen.

'Maybe I should leave,' whispered Diana.

'No, you're not leaving.'

'She's leavin' even if I have to drag her out myself.'

A familiar voice travelled from the bar, 'Do you have a problem Lieutenant Clarke?'

Bodies parted and sure enough Major Flatley and Commander O'Brien were sharing a drink, a comforting sight on his first visit.

'Enlisted are not permitted inside the officers club, unless she came to clean the latrine, sir.'

His fellow officers laughed at the jest, Flatley held a smug expression no thanks to Clarke's joke, 'You think you got what it takes to kick a Marine's ass, Lieutenant?'

'I can kick anyone's ass, and that's a fact, sir,' size was a great factor in inflating his ego despite a mere two weeks of basic combat training.

Flatley whispered to his first officer, 'I told you this was going to be good,' he stared at Diana, 'Private Zeng!'

She stood too attention, 'YES SIR!'

'At ease Private,' she relaxed, 'I'm ordering you to use whatever means necessary to remain inside these premises, do you understand?'

'UNDERSTOOD SIR!'

He smirked at Clarke, 'Clarke feel free to kick out Private Zeng, if you can.'

The blonde haired brute peered at Victor then back at the Major.

'No-one else is to intervene, is that understood?'

'YES SIR,' replied every officer in the bar, except O'Brien, he'd witnessed this more than once in his two centuries of training Space Force pilots.

Clarke moved on Diana like an eight hundred pound gorilla descending upon a delicate Asian butterfly. She a creature of elegance and grace ... he an unplotted brute grunting through flared nostrils, moving headlong to bash its opponent into submission. In a flash she leapt forward kicking him in the groin, male officers grimaced in pain, noise expressing Clarke's hurt rose above encouragement.

Flatley chuckled whilst sipping bourbon and branch water, female pilots started to get behind Diana as a red faced Clarke stumbled backwards into a table knocking over food and drinks.

Diana held her ground awaiting the next assault, following orders to the letter.

Clarke staggered to his feet, covered in beer and sauce, 'I'M GONNA KILL YOU BITCH!'

'Somebody got there first, numb nuts,' Diana revealed a deep neck scar beneath her collar.

Clarke stormed forwards, she dodged his first strike redirecting it, using Clarke's weight against him; a beastly Lieutenant embraced an unyielding metal wall. Clarke's full momentum contacted one of many large rivets ... square on his nose.

Diana stepped back within the club poised as a tiger waiting for Clarke's next assault. Clarke lay in a pool of blood and hot sauce at the exit. Male officers screamed for Clarke to get it together and kick her ass.

The utter shame of losing a fight to a woman half his size was too much to bare, Clarke rose with a bloodied and broken nose, a river of blood joined stains of mustard and barbecue sauce on his shirt. His eyes flicked to the floor, a broken beer bottle lay close by; Clarke squatted down and picked it up, 'I'll give you a matching pair bitch.'

Diana's hand moved inside her trouser pocket, in a fraction of a second the black point of her Fairbairn-Sykes combat dagger's beckoned Clarke on, 'And I'll cut your dick off, if you have one, loser.'

Again Clarke charged on his target, she moved as a panther on its prey , his undefined attack ... pathetic ... and Diana was being generous in her assessment. She'd have gone to harvesting if Murray witnessed technique that poor.

Clarke lunged forward with his broken bottle, before engaging her he'd put himself off balance. Diana kept her weapon close, slapped his uncoordinated attack away, her left hand reached up to his face gouging Clarke's eyes whilst pushing his head back and down, forcing the fellow's body to arch backwards. With her right hand Diana thrust her dagger into the front of his pants at full force several times

He hit the floor yelling in pain, she jumped on Clarke her blade surged toward exposed arteries on the neck. Like Flatley said you CAN die twice and Clarke's second passing approached … 'AT EASE PRIVATE ZENG!' bellowed the Major.

Diana stood up and sheathed her dagger whilst returning to Victor's side. Clarke rolled around the floor crying like a baby.

'Someone get this pussy ass flyboy to Medical.'

One of Clarke's fellow pilots hit his wrist sending a medical emergency call.

The Major rose from his barstool bourbon in hand, 'Anyone else think a Marine's not good enough to hobnob with you assholes?'

Silence prevailed. O'Brien mumbled under his breath, 'That's enough Jim.'

A team of Medics entered and rolled Lieutenant Clarke onto a gurney, 'My dick, she cut off my dick,' cried the blinded young man as he was carried off.

Major Flatley's evil spirit had been festering for centuries, every now and again he had to let the demon out otherwise it might consume any sanity that remained, 'Born on third base and think you hit a fucking home run, think you're all something special because you won the sperm donor lottery,' he took a deep slug of bourbon, 'I'm here to remind you that when you're flying around, flicking switches and discussing which year Dom Perignon you'll be drinking tonight, these guys are doing all the dirty work,' he pointed at Diana and Victor, 'you know why they're late to the party? Because they spent more than two years making Private; two thousand sent to harvesting and they still have another year on probation.'

Commander O'Brien grumbled in a hushed tone, 'Enough with the diatribe Jim.'

Flatley swung to face his friend, 'I'll say what I want, this is MY ship unless you're planning a mutiny?'

'No I'm not planning a mutiny,' he sighed.

Flatley returned to the pilots, 'When the enemy board your ship you better pray for the Marines, if he can't even bruise her you ain't got a fucking prayer against the Drax! Understood?'

'UNDERSTOOD SIR,' replied the pilots somewhat embarrassed by the Major's inebriated state.

O'Brien tried to calm Flatley down only to achieve the opposite effect. Diana stepped forward, 'Sir, permission to escort you to your cabin sir.'

Flatley looked at her then his glass of liquor, setting it down on the bar he pulled his tunic straight, 'Offer accepted.'

She guided him across broken glass and crockery to the exit; O'Brien gave a sigh of relief along with the rest of the officers club.

Flatley walked slowly along a corridor, Diana propped him up, 'You kicked his ass pretty good back there,' cackled the Major.

'Yes sir.'

'Tell me Zeng, what's going on between you and Zellmann?'

'We are friends, sir.'

He stopped and stared her in the face, 'Bullshit.'

'Sorry sir?'

'He's in love with you.'

'I do not know sir,' Diana peered at the floor.

'And you're in love with him.'

'Sir I think you need to rest now,' she tried to move on but he wouldn't budge.

'Are you in love with him Private?'

'Yes sir,' whispered Diana.

'You remember the resistance to interrogation examination?'

'Yes sir.'

'When you saw him get tortured?'

'Yes sir.'

'I could see it in your eyes, you cried and he went crazy when he saw what they did to you, but you both hung on because you knew the other would be there afterwards,' Flatley began to snivel.

Diana dragged him to his cabin as quickly as possible before anyone noticed. Back in the club Victor surveyed its menu, 'You guys eat food?'

'Sure,' replied O'Brien, 'something tickles your fancy?'

'It's been so long, we've only had liquid nanite drinks for sustenance.'

A female pilot ruffled her brow, 'You mean you've had nothing to eat in over two years?'

'Yeh.'

'Don't you have a menu in your Mess?'

'Yeh, just drinks … why do you eat food?'

'Well honey it's kind of like having sex, you don't do it just to procreate.'

At that moment Diana walked in to see female pilots standing around Victor, a mass of locusts descending upon a ripe crop. Unlike the defenceless farmer she moved in shooing away the voracious harpies, upon witnessing the short lady they retreated, 'Getting to know your fellow officers?' she stated in an upset tone.

'We were just discussing the menu here, do you want something?'

'I am pretty sure what they want and I wonder if it will be on the menu when I'm alone down below!'

'What are you talking about Dee?'

'Didn't you see them, they were about to eat you alive.'

He looked at the female pilots then back at Diana, 'You're overreacting.'

'Uuurrhhh, I never met a man that didn't follow either his belly or his cock, depending on which one is sticking out!'

'Why Diana Zeng, I do believe you're jealous,' he smiled as tears of passion welled up in her cold dead eyes. Victor took her by the hand to a quiet corner of the room, 'Take it easy Dee, I'm not interested in anyone else.'

'Maybe so, but they are interested in you.'

'Come on I want this date to be fun,' Victor raised a hand and a waiter delivered two hotdogs with fries, 'hungry?'

'They eat food in here?'

'She said it was like sex, you don't do it just to procreate.'

Diana put her hotdog back down to fix an iron stare on Victor.

'Okay maybe that wasn't the best analogy but you get the gist.'

She tasted the hotdog maintaining a matronly stare on her lover and superior. Sensations left forgotten for years detonated, the taste of food was painful at first, it never tasted so vibrant when alive. Ironic that only now could she appreciate vivid flavours ignored whilst alive, only in death did she recognise the intensity of life. Like a sudden flood of light it poured inside her soul creating an ocean she might launch then sail upon for a while.

Victor experienced similar explosions of pain then pleasure, how could a hotdog and French fries taste so good, they never tasted this good when catching a power lunch in New York. Its mustard burned, he couldn't tolerate more than a tiny dab. Those senses from the past made him think … had the Devil leased him this carcass just so he might accrue further sin, allowing his navigator, Charon, to plot a course deeper into hell. No, Victor was over analysing again, if he wasn't careful he'd end up like that French philosopher Diana talked about … what's his name? Ah yeh, Sartre, French and miserable with no friends. Even worse he might end up like Michaels, an insane man who'd mortgaged his soul to the Devil. Victor stopped thinking about it anymore, if he continued he'd realise how much he and Michaels actually had in common. The only thing preventing him falling into the same abyss as Sergeant Michaels was the beautiful woman sitting opposite.

After eating up and drinking two exquisite cokes their evening ended with a long walk. Before leaving the club Diana approached a gaggle of female officers chattering about tonight's mayhem, some slung over male pilots, 'Before I leave I want you sluts to know that he,' she pointed at Victor, 'is mine, anyone putting a finger on him gets a ticket to harvesting, understood?'

Victor burned with embarrassment as Diana threatened every female pilot with the equivalent of death in this new existence, traveling beyond Einstein's barrier.

Female pilots answered with silence.

'I'll take that as yes, do not disappoint me ladies,' she took Victor's hand and marched out the officers club.

They strolled until reaching a porthole where stars exploded in night's dark sheet, travelling faster than the speed of light.

'Thanks Dee, they'll all be making fun of me now.'

'You are a big boy, suck it up.'

'Why don't you trust me?'

'I trust you Vic, those dirty whores I do not trust, besides men think with either their …'

'Their bellies or their cocks, thanks for having such a low opinion of me.'

'Relax, you're a man, it's expected.'

'I'm sorry.'

'And stop saying sorry.'

'Did you enjoy the meal?'

'I did, but I enjoyed kicking Clarke's ass more.'

They embraced each other, 'I think that was definitely the high point.'

She looked at him with those glassy eyes, 'Do you love me Vic?'

'Of course I love you.'

'Do you love me so much that you wouldn't sleep with another woman, tell me the truth Vic.'

He brushed his fingers on her cheek, moved them down to touch her scar, 'Before I died I'd never felt true love.'

'Why?'

'I was married with the kids, she could take me to the cleaners. Moral guilt trips and financial threats kept us together more than anything else. In retrospect if I could just say to hell with it and leave her to live a bachelor existence I would've done it in a heartbeat.'

'I don't understand.'

'I paid lip service to love, like most men do. But here, with you, there are no guilt trips, no financial blackmail, no moving in with me and changing my life around or chasing off my friends. All those shackles that go with relationships have been shattered, now I can properly discern love from obligation. Only I can't let anyone know,' he looked her in the eye, 'except you Dee,' they kissed bringing necrotic flesh together as a star burst in then out of existence flooding the hall in a soft light, creating a sea for their passion to sail upon, if only for a few seconds.

Chapter Nine

Marines spoke in undertones before inspection. Victor's eyes met Michaels', 'Sergeant, why aren't you in the brig?'

'I was released, sir.'

Michaels' smirk burnt into Victor's psyche, 'We'll see Sergeant.'

'OFFICER ON THE DECK!'

Victor saluted toward the gantry. Flatley trundled out in a restrained fashion, 'AT EASE,' the Major reeled from his own voice.

Flatley activated a collar mic, preventing his brain from making further escape attempts, death was no cure for a hangover, 'Good morning … Marines … I'm as proud to say it as you are to hear it. Some of you had a little too much fun, as did I, so all sins are forgiven for one night.

Today is the beginning of the end, for the following thirty months you will continue training in planetary tactics and practice what you've already learned. I expect to see every one of you board S.S. Necron for active duty.

Out of two thousand six hundred and seventy three recruits, you made it. The hard part is over, only diligence remains … then maybe you'll get leave on one of those colonies you've all been gossiping about,' he winked and they laughed.

Flatley trundled off, propped against the hatch as he slowly exited. Victor turned around to see Sergeant Michaels' devilish grin, that smug son of a bitch was so pleased with himself Victor would've broke his knee caps if he could've gotten away with it.

That evening he and Diana strolled the outer decks arm in arm, 'I've never seen the Major like that before.'

'There was enough booze inside his cabin to open a sore,' replied Diana.

'I can't believe he let Michaels go, without even talking to me about it.'

'Come on, the man's a drunk, he probably thinks everyone else is too.'

Victor stopped walking, 'Don't talk about the Major that way.'

She pulled an incredulous expression, 'Why do you care? I mean it is not like you chose this life, death, you know what I mean.'

'Marines shouldn't talk bad about him, that's all.'

'What about speaking the truth, is that a problem?'

Victor sighed, 'He's the closest I have to a father now.'

'You still cannot recall your father?'

'No,' they continued to stroll, 'some memories won't come back, maybe I didn't know my father when I was alive, who knows?'

'You could look it up on your file.'

'He's not listed.'

'Oh, sorry Vic.'

'Don't be sorry, we've got the Marines for a family and I've got you. Tell me about your family, on Earth.'

'Not much more to say, I was born in Hong Kong. I had two sisters and a brother … he died in Hezhou after Triads tracked us down.'

'Why'd they kill you?'

'After Yankees nuked our coast large parts went untreated … the government called it affordable housing for the meagre, what they meant was a place to die for a destitute slave labour force. So we went to Necron and they took me.'

'Sounds like the West coast.'

She furrowed her grey brow, 'Didn't America clean it up.'

'It may have been one hundred years ago but you can see the West coast glowing from space. Where it set off the San Andreas Fault cities were just left to smoulder in radiation, government refused to pay for decontamination. Spending our tax rights … my tax rights on parties and picking fights in space somewhere!'

Diana hugged him tight, Victor always got mad about tax, probably because it's what got him into this situation, 'Sorry, Dee, go on.'

'Well they offered two contracts, I signed both and we moved from the fall out zone. Triads hunted us down, I died when they broke into our home, they were gonna kill us all, I tried to fight them off while my family escaped.

They got me and my brother before police arrived, I don't know what happened after but the money from Project Necron should help them get away.'

'What did they want you and your sisters for?'

'Drug runners and me for prostitution, rich customers check girls with a Geiger counter first, cannot have privileged pricks infecting wives with fallout!'

'I'm sorry.'

'Don't be … I killed one of those bastards before they held me down and cut my throat. So what's your story?'

'Ah, nothing interesting I got into tax arrears, was about to lose everything so signed up with Necron, the Doctor offered me a second contract and I took it.'

'Why didn't you pay tax?'

'The same middle class bullshit, holidays, cars, if the neighbours owned one ours had to be as expensive or more.'

Diana chuckled, 'Really?'

'By the time I told my wife no for the thousandth time that credit with an APR of 5000% started to look sweet, trust me.'

'Maybe you did it because you loved her.'

'That or I just wanted to shut her fucking mouth for a few hours!'

'Would you go into debt for me Vic?' she pouted her lips making a cute puppy dog face.

'I'm dead, I don't think my credit's good anymore.'

She slapped his side, 'That isn't fair.'

'Okay, okay, for you, I'd max out my credit rights … but for a holiday to Venus, you can kiss my ass!'

He tried to start walking again but she held him steady, 'What does that mean?'

'It means that if you really needed financial help I don't give a crap how much you need, it'd be yours. If you wanted a vacation to one up the neighbours, forget it honey.'

They continued down the hallway, 'I was wondering if you miss married life.'

'Yeh, just before I wake up in a sweat screaming for help.'

Diana laughed aloud, he kissed her head, 'You know we don't sweat or sleep Vic.'

'It's strange, being here is somewhat liberating, I don't have to pay tax, I don't have depressing legal responsibilities, no moral expectations. I'm free to love whomever I please and say whatever I want and losing you would put an end to whatever you call this excuse for an existence.'

'I love you too Victor.'

He peered down with a sly look in his eyes, 'How do I know you're not just saying that because you want preferential treatment from the LT?'

'Because you got the special thing when we were still recruits.'

'So it's my amazing charm and incredible good looks.'

The colour red emerged through the grey of death that usually held sway over Diana's face, 'And an inflated ego.'

'So why did you pick me?'

'I didn't pick you, your unit was next to mine. Besides we've met in a past life.'

'Not if I lived in New York.'

'Before that, I believe we have a spirit and live many lives.'

'So how do you explain this?'

'Maybe our spirits are trapped, trapped by science, but one day we'll expire and move on.'

'So you're saying our spirits haven't died yet.'

'No the spirit is eternal, trapped in our old body. We were together in another life and our spiritual bond brought us here together.'

'If you believe in that sort of thing.'

'What's your answer then?'

'I haven't got a clue, no-one can remember what came before birth so I guess no-one knows for sure what's after death, that's why we have religion.'

'You're one of those happy go lucky types?'

'Hey, I didn't say I don't like the idea of it, you know good guys go to heaven and bad guys go to hell ... that's a thought, maybe we died and went to hell?'

'Not possible.'

'How so?'

'No reality television.'

'I'll have to cede that point,' he looked into her warm opal eyes as she smiled back, 'Then we're in heaven.'

'That's a negative LT.'

'How's that?'

'First off the guy in charge has hangovers, second the next in command is an Irish Catholic.'

'What's wrong with being an Irish Catholic?'

'Jesus was Jewish numb nuts!'

'A minor technicality, I mean in two thousand six hundred years who's to say he hasn't considered another faith? There have been plenty of new ones and a few he probably didn't even know of at the time.'

'Nice try Vic but I won't take the bait that easily,' Diana being a spiritual person and Victor an atheist they clashed on the subject of religion as much as the subject of tax.

'Maybe he's a Buddhist or a Scientologist now?'

'Or maybe you are the second coming and testing me?'

'Ah yeh, I didn't think of that, risen from the dead, discovered by Diana Magdazen! Praise be!'

'You're not gonna make me angry that easy.'

'Hey you know how much Jesus likes that angry sex baby.'

'Kiss my ass Vic.'

Victor's eyebrows moved up and down upon his grey face in a cheeky manner, she slapped Victor's side broadening his grin. Diana looked around ... the corridor was deserted for now, she saw a toilet cubicle then yanked him over to it before closing its door behind them.

Flatley and O'Brien were chatting, the Major held a cup of iced coffee while walking off his hangover.

'I'd say you look like death, but ...'

'I feel like death ... with a throbbing head.'

'I bet Clarke has a throbbing head after that escapade you set up last night.'

Flatley snickered into a plastic cup.

'Fortunately his regeneration unit fixed him up.'

'Didn't lose his dick?'

'Oh she severed it off but the medics put it in a rib, the unit will merge the parts back together,' O'Brien held his hands out bringing them together to visualize the member's reconnection.

'Heh, heh, let's hope they put it in the right side up, otherwise he'll piss in his face the next time he goes to the latrine.'

'You gotta stop punishing my pilots, they're all good kids, it's not their fault they had an easy route.'

'You treat them too easy John,' he took some pills from his tunic pocket and swallowed them, 'ah, that's good coffee.'

'Two centuries on this ship, I don't know why I put up with your miserable ass Jim.'

'Because I got kicked off the Necron, that's why.'

'And pray tell, great one, why did thee get dropped from service?'

'That was Patterson.'

'You were caught drinking on duty.'

Flatley placed a grey palm against his head, the man in his mid-fifties groaned until pain dissipated, 'A couple of shots, maximum.'

'That's why Cliff got your job, he can't have a drunken first officer.'

'When did you become a Patterson fan-boy?'

'Just common sense, it's not like commanding the Necron is a simple task, you've been there in the thick of it, what if Patterson was drunk?'

'Patterson's an asshole.'

'Agreed, but nice guys don't command space cruisers.'

Flatley snorted.

'What?' snapped O'Brien.

'Unless they get shit out the right birth canal and daddy happens to be an Admiral.'

'Give it a rest Jim.'

'Give what a rest?'

'I ain't taking the bait, not this time!'

'Fine, then I'll just say it shall I?'

'You say what you want, it's your ship.'

'I'm on patrol, come home and Admiral Pratt's punk ass kid who washed out three times trying to land on a space carrier, THREE TIMES,' Flatley held his head reeling from a stinging pain, 'damn.'

'I think you need to calm down Jim.'

'I'll calm down when I see fit, anyway where was I?'

O'Brien sighed, he knew the story back to front by now, 'Washed out three times.'

'Right, he washes out three times, crashed into the fucking carrier even, now that's an automatic fail in itself. But he goes crying to daddy who just happens to be Admiral of the fleet and guess what?'

'Surprise me Jim,' stated O'Brien in a sardonic tone.

'He gets selected!'

'You don't say.'

'So I'm walking home, to surprise my wife and what do I see on the sofa, the sofa I got as a present from my brother on our anniversary, what do I see?'

'What did you see Jim?'

'Pratt's kid going up and down so fast his ass was approaching light speed!'

O'Brien snickered as Flatley became more animated splashing his coffee onto the floor, 'She screams, he gets up, nuts swinging in the wind and asks who the fuck am I? In my own fucking home!'

'Jim you'd been dead for six months, I'm surprised she didn't call for a priest.'

'Six months, is that what our marriage amounted to? Six months and she has some hotshot banging her brains out!'

'Shooting the Admiral's son was a bad move.'

'Ah, he lived, besides what would you have done?'

'I knew my wife was a slut before we got married. Anyway why would I want to turn up after she's buried me?'

'She's your wife.'

'Till death do us part.'

'Semantics.'

'You're dead and she's not, that's a fact. She moved on and thought you had until you turned up on the doorstep cap under arm. Perhaps you had justification in shooting that pipsqueak fucking your ex-wife but shooting her was a step too far, even for you.'

'It was a flesh wound!'

'That's not what they said at the trial.'

'That trial was bullshit and you know it, Pratt bribed the judge and hired the greasiest lawyers in town.'

'Necron Industries provided you with a pretty good legal team, look on the bright side … you got the sofa back.'

They stopped talking distracted by a banging noise rising and falling on the air as a mighty river flowing through a canyon, 'What the hell's that?' asked Flatley.

'Another coolant leak?'

'No,' they stood in silence listening to a regular thump against metal accompanied by feral grunts. Following the deep knocking Major Flatley and Commander O'Brien reached a closed cubicle door.

A few minutes passed before the door opened, Diana and Victor straightened their uniforms. She looked up through the exit's wicket posts to see Major Flatley and Commander O'Brien glaring back.

Diana jumped in fright then quickly saluted, Victor grumbled, 'Come on Dee what are you waiting for?'

'Is that you Lieutenant?'

Victor's head popped above Diana's, he stood to attention and saluted.

'Private Zeng, make way for the Lieutenant.'

She stepped outside, blocking Victor.

'Move to the side Private.'

She stepped to her left and there was Victor saluting his superiors in all his glory … trousers around his ankles.

'Good evening Lieutenant,' stated Flatley with a stone cold grimace, 'I and Commander O'Brien were chasing down a banging noise, I wonder if you heard it?'

'No, sir.'

'Private Zeng?'

'I heard no banging sir.'

'It was pretty loud, I reckon they heard it on the engineering decks, odd, very odd,' he peered at the Lieutenant's trousers, 'PULL UP YOUR PANTS LIEUTENANT!'

Victor dragged his trousers off the floor fastening them around his waist, 'Don't let me catch you with your pants down again Lieutenant, DISMISSED.'

'Yes sir,' the lovers scooted off like a pair of naughty school children.

Flatley and O'Brien waited until they were out of sight and burst into laughter.

'You can't beat angry sex,' chuckled Flatley.

O'Brien snickered, 'Is there any other way?'

Chapter Ten

A star hung in space, planets orbited at thousands of miles per hour, yet to the human eye still as night water on a lake. Within the scene a single square shaped craft, pocked with blocks seemingly a disorganized mess. Six large exhausts lighting the void with fires of Hephaestus. Its fore end displayed many long protrusions, pointing menacingly toward their goal as Ares spear moments before cast into the fray, felling heroes into a battlefield's blood caked dust. Sending warriors mourned by the living to the banks of the Styx where they might share tales of the war bringer and bemoan defying his mighty spear.

On this dark champion "S.S. NECRON" shone in bright white letters, a battlecruiser fit to serve as Ares mighty war chariot. Salvation to those who paid alms and tribute, ruination to fools poised in defiance before the bane of mothers, the most hated of Zeus' children, he whose rage shot fear into the hearts of men forcing many to flee the battlefield in search of sanctuary.

At Command and Control Commodore Ranulph Patterson leaned over a holographic representation of Tau Ceti. Necron's hologram threw out light casting shadows upon the ceiling, men and women worked in groups around its central projection some standing others sitting.

The Commodore wore his Royal Navy uniform, dark blue tunic, long sleeve white shirt with black tie. His shoulders shone, thick gold bars with a single gold circle above, twinkling as light from Tau Ceti's image bounced of them. A white topped cap with black peak, insignia of Necron Industries Navy stitched in gold cloth, an anchor set beneath a skull.

He'd served many years in the Royal Navy, commanding battleships and carriers, it was his life until his life ended. Ambushed off Proxima Centauri, fleet Admiral Cronin unaware his enemy orbited its star for weeks hiding themselves on the opposite side.

He'd waited for the enemy to burst out of light speed declaring himself as a parade band playing God Save the Queen. Instead he'd crept up using

Proxima Centauri's solar radiation as a cloak. By the time an alert went out and the order to scramble fighters was given the fleet were already under attack.

Despite best efforts his heavy battleship, the "Prince of Wales" was targeted for a nuclear strike. While his escape pod made its way through a debris field of British ships Patterson watched her last moments; her beautiful long sleek figure, the pride of his nations' fleet cracked and burned whilst Drax fighters moved in as a flock of vultures descending upon the plains of Africa. His enemy tore her wretched flesh piece by piece as men inside his pod prayed for deliverance.

He died from asphyxiation; fortunately for Necron the vacuum of space preserved their bodies perfectly. The company quickly accosted his corpse before it could be sent home; this was the beginnings of Project Necron.

Colonel Clifton Rockey was a Marine, cut from the same cloth as Flatley. Somewhere in his fifties on death, he made it in before Earth agreed to block Necron Industries. He and Flatley met on Parris Island, South Carolina, training for the U.S. Marines Corps, when one decided to try out for Special Forces the other followed. Two young men, no wives or children, they jumped at the chance to take a near light speed journey to Alpha Centauri.

It was on Alpha Centauri B Sergeant Rockey made Lieutenant, promoted in the grimmest fashion possible. There to seek out enemy camps around the U.S. colony, in the jungles of Alpha B soldiers died to Drax every day. Somehow they had information as to when and where they'd be beforehand.

After a couple of weeks Marines started to make headway until one night his base camp, protecting a civilian centre, was overrun. They charged from the tree line in droves like cockroaches running from fumigation. Alien shrieks and clicks haunt him to this today, a twisted noise hurtled towards his watch post, were they screaming in fear or encouragement, he still doesn't know.

Alien weapons fired bright bolts into darkness, men fell as ears of wheat, some ran others fought but most died. He and Flatley grabbed what they could and with their comrades fought for their lives.

An orbital strike hit, was it an enemy strike or friendly fire? Who knows? Who cares? The fact was he saw as many Drax die as men.

By the time dawn broke he and Flatley were not only alive but members of the officers club. He spent a decade defending Alpha Centauri until shipped back to Earth, he died from a heart attack at a strip bar … according to his wife it was the way he would've wanted to go.

Today he wore a black shirt and trousers, rank depicted on his shoulders by two white gold stars below a skull.

A Third man stood with them, he wasn't military, Dwight Connley was the company representative for Necron Industries, he wore a slick shiny two piece suit, pinstripe shirt, straight cut tie and very expensive Italian shoes. He constantly groomed his perfectly co-ordinated haircut with an ivory comb, most of the crew despised Connley yet he was the grease on Necron's war machine. Patterson didn't make a decision without Dwight's assessment beforehand, Necron was a business and the object of a business is to make profit. If you need assistance then first a deal has to be struck and until Dwight signs off on it there's no deal.

Dwight worked for Necron in his former life, before they found his body hanging by his bedsheets in a Frankfurt hotel. Deutsche Bank was on the edge of another default thanks to Dwight. He'd threatened not to rollover a large sum of bonds. Deutsche Bank didn't have the cash to pay him sparking a bank run and leading to a collapse of Bank shares, which Dwight held a short position on. He was extorting them, legally, for millions in Tax Rights. Major shareholders and the Executive board discussed their situation, in that pragmatic German fashion a conclusion was quickly reached, Dwight's early demise would solve many financial problems at the lowest cost.

Dwight's problem in life was that he was too good at extorting people, in death it was his grace.

'Commodore, S.S. Charon sighted, Sector zero, one, three, one, ETA fifty seconds.'

A clock lit up on the holo-map tagged to S.S. Charon's icon. It counted down as the icon approached Tau Ceti's star. All men and women aboard her remained in regeneration for the braking manoeuvre. Charon punched past the Necron in a streak of light throwing itself into orbit of Tau Ceti, captured by the star's gravity field, slowing the vessel down as main engines pointed forwards firing at full thrust.

Super computers calculated every single nuance of Tau Ceti's gravity well, pulling her below light speed whilst directing the Charon back toward the Necron.

Patterson watched the Charon fly into Tau Ceti's corona then disappear behind, seconds later she reappeared on the other side of Tau Ceti, a ball of fire hurtling toward them. Dwight's jaw dropped, he looked at the system map then the vessel moving toward them, 'They're gonna hit us!'

Patterson took a deep breath, 'ETA ten seconds … five, four, three,'

'Jesus they're gonna hit us!' yelped Dwight.

'Shut up!' snapped Patterson in his upper class accent.

'Two, one,' the Charon screeched to a halt only hundreds of kilometres from the Necron.

Dwight let out a great sigh of relief whilst checking the front of his pants. Colonel Rockey chuckled until Patterson's forbidding gaze shut him down.

'Sir we have made contact with the Charon, she's downloading cargo and crew manifest,' stated Petty Officer Brown from his station opposite Patterson.

'Send it to my cabin.'

'Understood Commodore.'

'Captain you have the Bridge,' he looked at Rockey, 'Your presence is required Colonel,' Patterson marched out of command with the Rockey in tow.

Ranulph's pencil moustache fitted his stiff manner as he marched down a corridor repressing a torrent of rage, 'I suppose you find this amusing Colonel?'

Rockey straightened his face, 'No sir.'

'You've always found that drunk and his school boy pranks amusing.'

'Major Flatley is not a drunk sir.'

'Major Flatley is not only a drunk but he is a mean drunk and we both know it.'

'It was fun watching Connley shit his pants.'

'Colonel, despite my loathing for that vile little excrement stain upon the underwear of humanity I am not amused. If I had moved the Necron from its designated rendezvous point by only a little we would be no more than radiation now.'

'Flatley knows you'd never move an inch from that point.'

Patterson came to a halt fixing his eyes on the Colonel, 'Suppose a Drax vessel had appeared, Colonel.'

He hung his head in capitulation, 'I understand, sir.'

'There's a reason Major Flatley is no longer an Executive Officer aboard this ship,' he carried on marching.

'That's not all his fault, sir.'

'Oh really Colonel? Do pray tell which part WAS his fault, drunk on duty or assaulting Mr Connley in the Command Centre?'

Rockey sneered, 'That pipsqueak had it coming.'

'Perhaps, but I cannot run this vessel with inebriated officers. This outrageous prank, endangering us all, proves that fact.'

Colonel Rockey rolled his eyes as he followed Patterson through a grey metal corridor.

On board the Charon men and women were dressed and packed, it was time to transfer into a new life or death, aboard the Necron.

Remaining men and women, Techs, Engineers, Pilots and Marines stood on Deck A carrying their possessions in a single sack. Six legs sprouted from the belly of their transport onto the deck, instead of wheels or skids, waiting to ferry them to the other side of the Styx.

'OFFICER ON THE DECK!' shouted Murray for the last time.

They stood to attention, 2nd Lieutenants, Sergeants, Corporals and Privates ready to leave, yet they would miss Murray and O'Brien after five years on the Charon.

'AT EASE,' shouted Flatley from his gantry, O'Brien by his side.

He scanned them, a band of motley recruits who didn't even know their identity five years ago, now the best in the universe … especially his Marines.

'When you first awoke you were nothing … today,' Flatley narrowed his vision onto his ninety three Marines, 'you're what makes the Drax afraid at night,' his Marines smiled with pride.

'You are the warriors on the edge of time, don't let me down,' with a tear in his eye he spoke his last words, 'DISMISSED!'

Men and women crammed into a transport, Flatley observed as its hatch closed, legs retracted, and shifted away past an energy barrier toward the Necron.

'That's another batch into the meat grinder Jim.'

'They'll do well.'

'How'd you know that?'

'Just a feeling.'

'Pah, long time since I had one of those!'

Flatley and O'Brien stepped off the gantry into a small shuttle.

'Looking forward to seeing your old friend Patterson?' said O'Brien.

'Like a rectal examination.'

O'Brien laughed slapping his legs.

'That guy's got such a plank up his ass.'

Commander O'Brien stopped laughing and peered beside him, 'Seems he'll be in good company.'

'You trying to say something?'

'Me? No, I'm sure Patterson's the only officer with a plank up his ass, a chip on his shoulder or a monkey on his back.'

Flatley pulled out a metal flask, flicked open its cap and took a swig, 'Drink?'

'Try restricting your thirst to revenge, if only for today.'

'I'm just getting started,' Major Flatley took another slug then rolled his lips back, 'Ahhhhh.'

A shuttle landed inside the Necron, its hatch opened, a set of steps folded out hitting the deck, 'Permission to come aboard.'

'Permission granted,' stated Rockey as his old friend stepped off onto Necron's polished flight deck.

Flatley and O'Brien approached the Commodore, both men saluted, Patterson returned their salute then offered his hand. He shook hands with Flatley to smell the powerful aroma of liquor, 'Good to see you Major.'

'It's an honour to be back on board, sir.'

'How are you Commander O'Brien,' he shook the Irishman's hand.

'Very well, sir.'

'How's this batch?'

'All up to standard, sir.'

He turned to Flatley, 'And the Marines?'

'Excellent batch, you got a good LT.'

'I certainly hope so Major, since nearly all Lieutenants are lost in their first engagement, Marines that is.'

'I guess life ain't so risky flying side saddle with barrage cannons covering your ass.'

Rockey held a sinister grin. O'Brien rolled his eyes, Patterson narrowed his and replied, 'Good to see you haven't changed Major. Perhaps you'd care to join us as we inspect the reinforcements?'

'Wouldn't miss it, sir.'

They strolled down the flight deck, a wide open space used for launching, landing and maintenance of all craft. High gantries right and left, maintenance trenches either side, one hundred metres down a transport unloaded its crew from the Charon.

Technicians, Engineers, Pilots and Marines separated into groups; Marines yet to be inspected by their Executive Officer Colonel Clifton Rockey, on his approach every Marine saluted. The old man was dressed in fatigues, ribbons lined his shirt, black beret displayed Necron Marines' white gold skull and crossed rifles glinting as powerful lights set within a lofty ceiling beamed upon them all.

'At ease assholes,' he walked up to Victor, 'Name.'

'Lieutenant Zellmann, Victor, serial number 02672, SIR!'

'Zellmann, you a kike boy?'

'No SIR!'

'You don't have to shout, I ain't deaf boy.'

'Yes sir.'

The Colonel approached Michaels, 'Name.'

'Sergeant Michaels, Broc, serial number 01990, sir.'

'Broc? Your papa name you after a vegetable or something?'

'It's Scottish, sir.'

'For what?'

Michaels avoided this for five years but Colonel Rockey had him cornered, 'Badger, sir.'

'I guess your papa liked you, 'cause if he hated you he'd have called you beaver!'

Some of the pilots laughed but Marines stared forward in silence, going with the Colonel's powerful current.

Rockey continued along the first row, 'Name.'

'Corporal Mercer, Terrence, serial number 01821, sir.'

'Another nigger, how come you signed up for Project Necron?'

'I thought it said, Project Negro, sir.'

Rockey chuckled then quickly lost his humour, 'I'M THE ONLY COMEDIAN HERE, YOU UNDERSTAND BOY?'

'YES SIR!'

Colonel Rockey moved down the ranks halting at Diana, 'Name.'

'Private Zeng, Diana, serial number 02673, sir.'

He took out a tablet, brought up the roster then her file, 'Only female to make it, so who'd ya stab in the back to get here?'

'No-one sir.'

'DAMN SLANTY EYED BASTARD,' with the other hand he pulled his combat knife, in a fraction of a second its cold metal pressed on Diana's throat, the entire deck was suspended in time, Diana didn't twitch.

Colonel Rockey waited for a reaction, when none was forthcoming Clifton sheathed his blade then returned to the Commodore, 'Inspection over sir.'

Patterson stood before his Marines, Navy tunic and tie smartly pressed, 'I am Commodore Patterson and you are now property of the S.S. Necron. Amongst Marines only the exceptional enter active duty, in turn I expect exceptionality. Colonel Rockey is Executive Officer responsible for Marines on board this vessel, all day to day and tactical decision are deferred to him. Impress Colonel Rockey and you shall impress me.

I see some are keen to enter the fray, have no fear your time will come. Until then remember you are members of my crew so carry yourselves with dignity and honour, that will be all, dismissed.'

The men broke up making their ways to barracks, Victor to his own cabin on the officers' deck. Unpacking his gear into a locker he checked the room, similar to his quarters on the Charon, it sufficed. He saw himself in a mirror above a small wash basin, grey eyes, gaunt face, Lieutenant Victor Zellmann smiled back in congratulation.

There was a thud on the door, 'Hey Vic, you home?'

His hatch opened and she walked through, the love of his death, Victor saw vibrant colour in her smiling eyes. Diana's spirit forced emotion into the universe, his lifeless husk fortunate to be its focus, as a sail catching a sea breeze Diana pushed him toward foreign lands so he might embrace love on her shores.

'Nice digs.'

Victor placed his arms around her, 'Even better now you're here.'

Examining the room she noticed herself in the mirror and quickly turned away.

'What's up?'

'I don't like mirrors.'

'How come?'

'Another time.'

Before he could inquire further a flash of light attracted them to the porthole. The Charon departed, using Tau Ceti as a sling shot she catapulted herself back to Earth in a streak of fire. Just as an aeroplane creates a boom on breaking the sonic barrier the Charon caused an explosion of white light on breaking Einstein's barrier, passing from near light to super light speeds, it bathed Victor's cabin in bright white light. In five years Flatley would be back home orbiting Earth, five minutes from Victor's perspective.

They kissed pressing against one another, he whispered through her auburn hair into a cold ear, 'Our whole relationship was only five minutes for these people.'

'The best five minutes I ever had,' replied Diana kissing him again as their former home passed beyond Einstein's barrier.

The End